My Epic Spring Break (Up)

Also by Kristin Rockaway

The Wild Woman's Guide to Traveling the World

How to Hack a Heartbreak

She's Faking It

My Epic Spring Break (Up)

Kristin Rockaway

Underlined

All rights reserved. Published in the United States by Underlined, an imprint of Random House Children's Books, a division of Penguin Random House LLC, New York.

Underlined is a registered trademark and the colophon is a trademark of Penguin Random House LLC.

GetUnderlined.com

Educators and librarians, for a variety of teaching tools, visit us at RHTeachersLibrarians.com

Library of Congress Cataloging-in-Publication Data
Names: Rockaway, Kristin, author.
Title: My epic spring break (up) / Kristin Rockaway.
Other titles: My epic spring breakup
Description: First edition. | New York : Underlined, [2021] | Audience: Ages 12 and up. |
Summary: When coder extraordinaire Ashley's well-defined college prep plans veer off course, she decides to have fun during spring break and, for the first time, follow her heart.
Identifiers: LCCN 2020023389 (print) | LCCN 2020023390 (ebook) |
ISBN 978-0-593-18011-2 (trade paperback) | ISBN 978-0-593-18012-9 (ebook)
Subjects: CYAC: Dating (Social customs)—Fiction. | Computer programming—Fiction. |
High schools—Fiction. | Schools—Fiction. | Family life—New York (State)—New York—Fiction. |
New York (N.Y.)—Fiction.
Classification: LCC PZ7.1.R63952 My 2021 (print) | LCC PZ7.1.R63952 (ebook) |
DDC [Fic]—dc23

The text of this book is set in 12-point Adobe Garamond.
Interior design by Ken Crossland

Printed in the United States of America
10 9 8 7 6 5 4 3 2 1
First Edition

For the kids on the math team,
and for the kids on the literary magazine,
and, especially, for the kids on both

Chapter One

Growing up in New York City is a crash course in the art of self-defense. I don't mean learning martial arts or the proper way to use a stun gun or anything like that. I mean quickly and accurately assessing people and situations for potential disasters so you can avoid them before they happen.

That discounted MetroCard someone's trying to sell you on the street? It's a scam.

That guy sitting in the corner of the subway car, making kissy noises and hissing in your direction? Don't make eye contact.

That one lonely cockroach you saw zooming across your kitchen counter the other day? It's *never* one lonely cockroach. Trust me when I say there's a million more where that came from. Have your parents call the landlord, pronto.

Basically, if you want to survive (and keep your apartment vermin-free), you need to know trouble when you see it.

And I know trouble when I see it.

This morning, trouble takes the form of Jason Eisler, strolling into American History with a goofy grin and an easy stride.

On the surface, there's nothing concerning going on here. Just a teenage boy rolling into class, hands in the pockets of his hoodie, backpack bouncing with each step.

But I know Jason too well not to be concerned. There's a certain subtle glimmer he gets in his brown eyes when he's up to no good. The first time I remember seeing it, we were in second grade, and he'd somehow managed to sneak a life-like rubber tarantula into our teacher's top desk drawer. When poor Ms. Chen opened it up, she went paler than Marsh-mallow Fluff, shrieking so loudly that one of the girls at table two started to cry. Five minutes later, the principal showed up in our classroom, his bushy eyebrows furrowed with disdain as Ms. Chen explained what happened. Jason wasn't fazed, though. He just giggled, eyes glimmering, as he followed the principal out the door.

In the intervening decade, Jason's pranks have become more sophisticated, more interesting, but that glimmer in his eyes is still the same. It dances a little now when he looks my way.

"What's up, Ashley?" he calls from the front of the room. People turn to check me out, but I slide farther down in my chair and glare at the scratched desktop. I want no part of whatever he's got planned.

The bell chimes to signal the start of the period, and five seconds later, Ms. Henley closes the classroom door. "Take your seats, please," she says. After everyone settles in, she projects a slideshow about the Cuban Missile Crisis onto the whiteboard. You'd think she'd go easy on us since it's the last day of school before two weeks of spring break, but that has never been Ms. Henley's style.

"Today we're going to discuss the role diplomacy played in . . ." Her voice trails off when the door squeaks open, and

I think I see a thin curl of smoke wafting from each of her nostrils. Ms. Henley *hates* latecomers. Her shoulders hunch toward her ears, and I can tell she's preparing to lay into this unfortunate soul with a tirade about time wasting and personal responsibility. But when she sees who it is, her shoulders relax again.

It's Walker Beech, the opposite of trouble.

He looks appropriately contrite. "Sorry I'm late, Ms. Henley."

"It's okay, Walker." She waves away his apology with a casual smile. "We were just getting started."

Only Walker Beech could elicit such a warmhearted response from the iciest teacher at Edward R. Murrow High School.

As Walker slips inside and gently closes the door behind him, I try not to stare. It's no use, though. His body's like a magnet dragging my attention away from Ms. Henley, who's now gesturing toward a map of Cuba. She's droning on about the Bay of Pigs, but all I can focus on is Walker's hair, the way his thick brown curls defy gravity. I wonder if he spends a lot of time getting them so flawlessly tousled or if it's a natural phenomenon. Probably the latter.

At least I'm not the only one distracted by his magnificence. From my vantage point in the middle of the classroom, I can see at least three other people—Chelsea, Yaritza, Marcus— watching his every move. Their heads turn in unison, tracking him as he walks down the fourth row of desks, headed for the empty seat directly to my left.

Omigod.

He's sitting next to me.

In one motion, I sit up straight and tuck my hair behind my ears, smoothing any flyaways. Not that he's looking at me or anything. As he passes me, I get a whiff of his cologne. It smells like one of those clove-scented oranges Mom sets around the table at Christmastime.

The moment he slides into his chair, he's already engrossed in the lesson, notebook open to a blank sheet of paper, pen uncapped, ready to write. He squints his hazel eyes at the whiteboard, clearly fascinated by Ms. Henley's discussion of geopolitical strife at the height of the Cold War.

So dreamy. So mysterious.

That's the thing about Walker Beech—the thing that makes him the opposite of trouble. He's always attentive in class, always completely respectful. I didn't know him in second grade, but I'm certain he never hid a rubber tarantula in his teacher's top desk drawer.

Okay! Enough obsessing over Walker Beech.

As I'm finally tuning in to Ms. Henley's monotonous speech, I'm distracted yet again. This time by Jason, who's fidgeting in his chair, shifting awkwardly with his arms folded across his chest. I'm sure he's uncomfortable sitting in the front row, right under Ms. Henley's nose, but it's not like he has a choice in the matter. Those fart noises he made on the first day of the semester earned him the distinct honor of being the only person in class with an assigned seat.

No one else seems clued in to Jason's restlessness, but that's not a surprise. Like I said, I know him really well.

And I know when he's hiding something.

Right now, that something appears to be shiny and cylindrical and candy-apple red, because I see the end of it slipping out the bottom of his hoodie. He shifts again and it disappears. Behind him, Dmitry Yablokov props his phone up on his desk, angled beside his binder so Ms. Henley can't see it—if she did, it would be locked in her file cabinet in two seconds flat. When he sets the video and slides his thumb to the record button, alarm bells go off in my head.

Trouble.

Sure enough, Jason gets to his feet.

"Sit down, Mr. Eisler." Ms. Henley's voice is sharp but exasperated. Predictably, Jason acts as if he hasn't heard her.

He turns to face the class, one hand waving in the air, the other one reaching behind his back, presumably keeping that shiny, cylindrical, candy-apple-red thing from falling out beneath his hoodie. A few giggles echo around the room. Several people suck their teeth.

"Guess what, everybody?" he yells. "It's my birthday!"

It isn't his birthday. Today is March 25, and he turns seventeen on April 10. But this bald-faced lie isn't the biggest problem at hand.

Ms. Henley knows it, because she sighs and pushes her glasses up onto her head. When she pinches the bridge of her nose, her eyes close just long enough to miss the moment when Jason whips out the cylinder. It's about two feet long, with the words PARTY POPPER emblazoned on the side.

A confetti cannon.

This should be fun.

"Let's have a party!" he yells.

A split second later, there's a deafening crack. Ms. Henley shrieks, sounding exactly like Ms. Chen did in the second grade. The classroom is showered with colorful tissue paper. It flits through the air, glittering in the fluorescent overhead lights, pink and blue and silver and gold. It lands in our hair, on our clothes, all over our desks and the floor. Our boring social studies lesson has been transformed into the grand finale of a Taylor Swift concert.

It's actually kind of magical. I can't help smiling.

Everyone else is smiling, too, even the people who were sucking their teeth ten seconds ago. Chatter and laughter erupt. A few daredevils reach for their phones, but Ms. Henley immediately puts the kibosh on that.

"Don't even think about taking pictures or I'll lock up your phones until you return from spring break!"

Dmitry's phone is already out of sight. He's all innocence and wonder now, playfully tossing handfuls of confetti at Rachel Gibbons, as if he hadn't been the designated cameraman for this spectacle.

I wonder how Jason convinced him to do it. Probably cash. All those hours Jason spends stocking shelves with me at the ShopRite, only to throw it away making these videos.

See, last year Jason decided to broaden his audience and expand his reach from our overstuffed Brooklyn high school to the entire world—or, at least, to anyone with internet access. He has dreams of going viral.

Lately, these videos have taken over his life. He doesn't participate in a single legitimate extracurricular activity—you know, something he can list on his college applications. Me? I'm a peer math tutor, a Mathlete, and a member of the Coding Club. And while I do enjoy these extracurriculars, I also chose them very deliberately, to show prospective universities how serious I am about pursuing a STEM degree. They're strategic moves.

Jason never does anything strategically.

Case in point: the current debacle in our confetti-covered classroom.

"Unacceptable!" Ms. Henley's face is as red as the now-empty cardboard tube dangling from Jason's right hand. "You'll be lucky if you don't get expelled!"

"For a few scraps of tissue paper?"

Her face grows redder still. "In this day and age, Mr. Eisler, the sound of a firecracker is not to be taken lightly, particularly inside a school. The threat of violence is real, and it is no laughing matter!"

For the first time, his confidence wavers. I can tell because the glimmer is gone and his lips twitch the tiniest bit. Imperceptible to most; unmistakable to me.

"But I wasn't threatening anything," he says. "I was just—"

"To say nothing of the mess you've created in my classroom!"

She's breathing heavily now, the wheeze of her smoker's lungs audible from halfway across the suddenly silent room. Jason's lips twitch again, and I wonder if maybe he's feeling a twinge of regret.

I steal a glance at Walker, but he doesn't seem to care about the drama unfolding before our eyes. Instead, he's looking down at his lap, where his thumbs tap frantically against his phone screen.

It's a bold move to be texting in Henley's class. Then again, she's dealing with more pressing matters right now, and Walker's discreet. He may be breaking the rules, but it's a quiet, clever defiance.

Walker Beech is strategic.

"You know what?" Jason says. "You're right. I didn't realize there was gonna be so much confetti in this thing. Lemme run to the custodian's office real quick to grab a broom so I can clean it up."

Ms. Henley looks personally offended. "Oh no. You're going to the dean, immediately." She walks over to the wall-mounted landline beside the door and jabs at the keypad. "I'm calling him now so he knows to expect you."

As she grouses into the handset, Rachel Gibbons calls out, "Happy birthday, Jason!"

Just like that, the glimmer in his eyes is back.

Rachel knows it's not really his birthday. At least, she *should* know—she's his ex-girlfriend, after all. They dated for eight months, from the end of last school year until the beginning of January. I'm tempted to call her out on it, but then I realize she might be in on this prank. She's the whole reason he decided to start recording these videos in the first place.

Soon the whole class starts singing the birthday song. I don't want to seem like a wet blanket, so I mumble along. Then Ms. Henley slams the phone back on the wall and spins around. "Quiet down!" The singing ends abruptly. She points one stubby finger toward the door and glares at Jason. "Dean Ross is waiting for you, Mr. Eisler. I suggest you leave immediately."

"Will do." He slings the cardboard tube over his shoulder like a hobo stick and turns to leave. With his hand on the door-knob, he pauses and looks back at me, the glimmer dancing in his eyes.

"Out!" Ms. Henley shrieks, and he's gone.

If the prank itself was the finale of a Taylor Swift concert, then the present moment is fifteen minutes after the encore, when the lights are too bright and the floor is a mess and you're trapped in a bottleneck of hundreds of people trying to cram themselves through a few narrow stadium doors. The mundane reality of life is painful after such an extravagant show.

Maybe Ms. Henley feels the same way. Maybe the silver lining on this confetti cloud is a temporary reprieve from history class. With all the excitement—not to mention the mess—surely there's no way we could be expected to continue with this lesson.

"Don't think you're getting out of this lesson!" Ms. Henley sweeps a few stray pieces of tissue paper off her laptop and taps the trackpad. On the whiteboard, the map of Cuba is replaced with a bullet-pointed list of keywords beside a black-and-white photo of JFK. "I'll clean this all up after the period's over. Right now, it's back to work."

So much for a silver lining.

Everyone settles down so Ms. Henley can resume her lecture, but I'm too amped up to concentrate. There's a buzzing in my ears, almost like I'd actually been to a concert, and my brain feels fuzzy. Even if I was interested in the intricacies of the Cold War, I probably couldn't process a word coming out of Ms. Henley's mouth right now.

My eyes slide to Walker, who's back to being focused and disciplined. Notebook open, pen at the ready, phone nowhere to be seen. Ever the opposite of trouble.

Not for the first time, I wonder what his hair feels like. Is it soft and silky, or sticky with product? If I sank my fingers into those thick, brown curls, would they slide through easily or get tangled up in knots?

And I just now noticed: his hands are *impeccable*. Square palms. Strong knuckles. Clean, trim fingernails. He grips his ballpoint pen with purpose as it glides across his college-ruled paper. I can't see what he's writing, but I'm sure his notes are insightful interpretations of whatever Ms. Henley is blathering about.

Suddenly, his pen stops moving, which is weird because Ms. Henley's still talking. My gaze drifts upward from his hand to his face and oh god those hazel eyes are aimed right at me.

I've been caught staring.

This is a *disaster*.

My brain screams, *Look away, Ashley!* But I can't. The magnetic force of his body has pulled me in.

His brows knot together—confused, amused, who can tell?—and then the corners of his perfect mouth turn up. I'm not sure if he's laughing at me or with me, but I do know this is the first time he's ever looked at me. Like, *really* looked at me.

My breath comes fast and shallow, and when Walker drops his pen on his notebook, I stop breathing altogether. Because his impeccable hand is reaching across the aisle, and now it's in my hair, and it's possible I may pass out from lack of oxygen.

When he pulls his hand away, there's a slender scrap of pink paper pinched between his thumb and forefinger. He shows it to me with a smile, then lets it flutter to the floor.

Immediately, he resumes his note-taking, but I'm not even in the classroom anymore. I'm at the finale of a Taylor Swift concert.

No, scratch that. I'm in Times Square on New Year's Eve. The ball's just dropped and everyone's cheering and confetti is flying around like magic pixie dust.

Walker Beech touched me.

There's my silver lining.

Chapter Two

I still have a contact high from Walker Beech's fingertips when I walk into Coding Club after school. It's a small club, twelve members in all, which is pitiful considering there are nearly four thousand students enrolled at Murrow. Earlier this year, we tried to recruit more people, but the flyers wc so carefully hung in the hallways and distributed at lunchtime became quick ammunition for paper-snowball fights. The custodian lodged a complaint with the principal, who subsequently banned all clubs from handing out flyers.

After that, we gave up recruitment efforts. If people don't want to learn to code, I suppose that's their prerogative.

It's their loss, though, because not only does Coding Club look great on a college application, it's also a lot of fun. Our staff adviser, Mr. Podonsky, lets us hang out in his workshop, gives us general guidance, and answers our questions when we get stuck. And we always get to pick the kinds of projects we work on. We've made some really cool stuff so far this year, like a custom calendar app that syncs with our bell schedule, and a meme generator that features photos we snagged from the yearbook.

Right now, we're focused on wearables—tech you can wear on your body—and we've split into our usual groups of two or three people per project. I always sit with my friends Christine Kong and Heaven Ruiz, who are already set up at the small round table in the back of the classroom when I arrive.

As I slide in beside them, Heaven looks up from her laptop. "What are you smiling about?"

I plonk down my backpack, ready to relay the story of the confetti cannon and my close encounter with Walker, but Christine interjects with an excited, "Omigod! Did you get in?"

"No." My shoulders slump slightly. "Not yet, anyway."

She's talking about the internship I applied for at ZigZag. ZigZag's the hottest new social media platform: think Instagram, Snapchat, and TikTok all rolled into one. This summer, they're offering an all-expenses-paid, six-week immersion program at their headquarters in Silicon Valley, and I'm dying to be a part of it.

The summer between junior year and senior year is the ideal time to boost your college applications. Heaven's doing a job shadow at a civil-engineering firm in Manhattan, and Christine's heading out to New Haven for a study program at Yale. I'm the only one who hasn't solidified my summer plans yet, but with my GPA, extracurriculars, and solid letters of recommendation, I feel like I have an extremely good chance of being accepted to ZigZag. In fact, I think I may be a shoo-in.

To be perfectly honest, I'm not a huge ZigZagger. Even though I scroll through the feed a lot, my follower count isn't very high and I don't post all that often. But ZigZag is the only tech firm in Silicon Valley to offer a fully funded residential summer internship for rising high school seniors. And since my ultimate goal in life is to become a software engineer and dominate Silicon Valley, I need to get my foot in the door as soon as possible.

Plus, experience as a ZigZag intern will undoubtedly impress college admissions officers. After all, that's what high school is really all about: prepping for college. My top choice is Stanford, followed closely by UC Berkeley. Really, though, any university with a prestigious computer science department will do.

Decision letters for the internship are going out any day now. I've been refreshing my email incessantly, always feeling a stab of disappointment whenever the answer isn't waiting for me in bold letters at the top of my in-box. I'd managed to put it out of my mind for the duration of Ms. Henley's class, but the urge to check my email has suddenly returned.

"Then what is it?" Heaven asks.

Compared to the enormity of being accepted into the Zig-Zag program, the real reason for my smile feels stupid and irrelevant. Walker Beech plucked a piece of confetti from my hair. So what? He doesn't even know my name.

Before I can answer, Mr. P stands in front of the classroom and gestures for everyone's attention. "Excuse me. Just a quick question before you get too involved in your work. Show of hands: how many people have already registered for the spring break hackathon?"

A bunch of us raise our hands, including me and Christine. Heaven doesn't, though. She's going to Puerto Rico to visit her grandma during the second week of spring break, and she's looking pretty surly about it right now.

"I can't believe I'm missing it," she says, her lower lip pushed into a sad little pout.

"It's not gonna be that great," I say.

Truth is, though, it *is* gonna be that great.

The New York City High School Spring Break Hackathon is a marathon coding competition held at the NYU School of Engineering, open to all ninth through twelfth graders in all five boroughs. It's essentially twenty-four hours of brainstorming ideas and developing software. The judges present a technical challenge and give you a whole day and night to come up with an innovative solution. They welcome all levels of coders, from beginner to advanced. Of course, you have an advantage if you know how to code.

Naturally, I plan to win.

"If you haven't signed up yet," Mr. P says, "it's okay. You can still register up until the night before. However, they expect you to bring your own laptop, so if you need to borrow one from the workshop here, you're welcome to do so. They're already preloaded with all the software you could possibly need. You'll just have to sign one of these laptop checkout agreements on my desk.

"Aside from that, you may want to bring a sleeping bag if you plan on catching some *Z*s. But from what I've seen at these hackathons, most people stay up all night to perfect their projects."

Christine and I exchange a smile. We've formed our own little team of two. Heaven still looks pretty sulky, and I don't blame her. It stinks that she's going to miss it.

Mukesh asks, "What are the prizes this year?"

"They haven't announced them yet," says Mr. P. "They haven't announced the judges yet either, but it's probably going to be some combination of tech professionals and academics."

After Mr. P concludes his speech, I head over to his desk to sign one of the laptop checkout agreements. It lists all sorts of rules and restrictions for acceptable use and proper care—don't leave it in an unsecured area, don't lend it out to anyone, don't use it to surf shady websites. All pretty basic stuff.

As I ink my name at the bottom of the page, Mr. P asks, "Are you excited for the hackathon, Ashley?"

"Yes, very," I say.

"Who's on your team?"

"It's just me and Christine."

He nods. "You're both strong coders, but you *can* have up to four people on your team. Part of the fun of a hackathon is meeting new people, and you can easily join forces with some other participants once you're there. The more people on your team, the better your chances of winning."

"Thanks for the tip," I say, then grab a laptop from the storage cart and return to my table, where I pull my wearable project from my backpack: a light-up hoodie. I've already sewn LEDs across the chest and along the sleeves using conductive thread. Now all I have to do is write instructions to make them blink in time to music.

Christine glances at my handiwork. "That's looking really good so far."

"Thanks." Though I'm not completely thrilled with it. Before this project, I'd never picked up a needle and thread, so my stitches are uneven, and a couple of the LEDs are slightly askew. I glance at the pendant around her neck and say, "Yours looks great. How's it coming along?"

"Not bad." She taps her laptop keyboard and the pendant glows bright red.

"Cool!" I say.

Heaven nods approvingly. "That looks like something out of a sci-fi movie."

Another tap and the pendant goes dark. "I'm trying to get it to change color based on the temperature. Red if it's hot, green if it's cool, blue if it's cold."

"Awesome."

I'm about to ask Heaven how much progress she's made on her remote-controlled tiara, but she's already perched it atop her curls. "Check it out," she says, and swipes her thumb across her phone screen. Instantly, the LED "jewels" in her crown shine brightly like white diamonds. "Next, I'm gonna add voice control. Make it light up when you say 'All hail, Queen Heaven.'"

Christine and I can't hold back our laughter. Of course Heaven would create a wearable that got people to call her Queen.

"I wish I was doing the hackathon with you guys," she says, untangling her hair from the teeth on the sides of her tiara.

"Well, I wish we were going to Puerto Rico with you," I say. "The hackathon is gonna be fun and everything, but I'd much rather spend my spring break in a tropical paradise."

"Trust me, my grandma's house is not a tropical paradise."

I flip a switch to illuminate my hoodie. These crooked LEDs are bugging me, and it looks even worse now that it's lit. Holding it up for the girls to inspect, I ask, "Does this look bad?"

They both squint, like they're trying to figure out what I'm talking about. Christine says, "No, it looks fantastic."

"Really?" I point out the most egregiously lopsided LED. "This one's all wonky. I think I'm gonna take out the stitches and start again."

Heaven grimaces. "You're crazy. That took you, like, hours to sew into place."

"Yeah, but if I don't fix it, it'll always bother me." I grab scissors from the center of the table and start snipping. "I want it to be perfect."

"There's no such thing as perfect." Christine tosses out this nugget of wisdom as if it's an absolute truth.

"I beg to differ," Heaven says, tossing her curls over her shoulder in a flourish of self-confidence. "You're looking at perfection right here."

Christine rolls her eyes and we both giggle. "All hail, Queen Heaven," I say, then pull a long strand of connective thread out of my hoodie. The LEDs pop off and I begin the arduous task of sewing them back in, one by one, until they look totally perfect.

Chapter Three

An hour later, I'm waiting at the bus stop under the elevated subway station on Avenue M. My shoulders ache from the weight of my backpack, and I can't wait to get home and change into my fuzzy pajamas. Spring break is finally here, and I want to celebrate by getting cozy.

As usual, the bus is late, though it's not like public buses in Brooklyn ever run according to schedule. It feels like I've been standing here forever, so I step off the curb and stand in the street, searching for signs of an approaching B9.

Then someone calls my name, and I turn to see Jason emerging from a convenience store. He yells "Catch!" and chucks something my way. I run back to the sidewalk in time to catch a packet of Mentos, the fruit kind I love. I'm amazed he remembers. It's been months since we shared a roll of these. Maybe even a year.

"Thanks." I peel back the wrapper and pop one off the top before handing it back to him.

He waves me off. "Take the whole thing, they're for you. Why are you still hanging around?"

"Coding Club ended a little while ago," I say, slipping an orange candy into my mouth. It took the entire period to finish sewing on the LEDs, but they line up perfectly now. "Why are *you* still hanging around?"

His eyes fall to the cracks in the pavement. "Ross kept me after school. He gave me some big, long lecture and called my parents. Now I'm grounded. As soon as I get home, I gotta turn in my phone. My dad's not giving it back to me until Monday morning."

It's not as bad as an expulsion, but it's still a big deal. No one wants to lose their lifeline, especially over the weekend. "Was it worth it?"

"I don't know yet. Dmitry posted the video about an hour ago, so it depends on how many views we get."

He takes a big swig from his can of Coke and I shake my head in exasperation. "You're lucky you didn't get in bigger trouble."

"Pssh." Jason smirks, suddenly brimming with confidence. "There's no way they could've expelled me over that. Henley doesn't know what she's talking about."

"Doesn't it ever get old?"

"Doesn't what ever get old?"

"Pulling pranks like that."

"No. Why would it? It's fun. Everyone except Henley loved it. You were smiling, too, so don't act all high and mighty."

He's right, of course. With all that confetti swirling around, I'd gotten lost in my Taylor Swift concert fantasy. Even before Walker plucked the tissue paper out of my hair.

Omigod, Walker Beech touched me today.

"See?" Jason says. "You're smiling now just thinking about it."

"I'm thinking about something else."

"Yeah, okay." He chugs the rest of his soda and sets the can on the edge of an overflowing trash bin. "I know you love my pranks, Ashley. You always have."

As much as I don't want to admit it right now, I *have* always loved his pranks.

I can't remember a time when I didn't know Jason. We've lived in the same apartment building practically since birth, we've been classmates since kindergarten, and our moms are really good friends. Our lives have always been intertwined by circumstance.

A few years ago, though, we started hanging out together by choice. The summer after eighth grade, with nothing else to do, we spent a lot of time bumming around the neighborhood. We'd get Carvel sundaes for lunch and sit on the benches at the Ocean Parkway Malls. Sometimes we'd go on Pokémon Go hunts at the cemetery. On really hot days, we'd play Xbox in Jason's blissful air-conditioned living room.

But the highlight of that summer, by far, was watching Jason pull the most epic pranks. He glued pennies to the sidewalk and gave random high fives to strangers. He followed runners around Gravesend Park while blasting "Eye of the Tiger" on his phone. Once, he rigged an air horn to honk whenever someone opened the door to our building's parking garage.

I was never an active participant in his pranks, just a spectator, standing off to the side and laughing while he did his thing. Sometimes I'd help him prepare. Every moment was unpredictable and exciting. I quickly became his number one fan.

Then, last year, he started dating Rachel Gibbons.

Their relationship didn't exactly come out of nowhere. I knew he liked her. One day, she showed up at school with these long pink streaks in her dark brown hair, and he said to me, "Rachel looks hot."

Admittedly, her hair did look cool. Rachel always looks cool no matter what she's doing. That's why she has thousands of ZigZag followers.

Still, his comment annoyed me. Then he asked me if I had a thing for anybody at school and I said no, even though I'd been harboring this crush on Walker for months already. I just didn't want Jason to know. I don't know why.

Anyway, then they started dating, and Jason and I stopped hanging out. He spent all his free time with Rachel, and she replaced me as his number one fan. She was better at it, too, since she encouraged him to record these videos and set him up with a ZigZag channel.

I have to say, though, once Rachel got involved, I stopped loving his pranks so much.

"Bus is coming," Jason says, and sure enough, there it is, lumbering down Avenue M. From a block away, I can see it's standing room only. At least a dozen other people are waiting at this stop, too, so who knows if we'll even get on.

"Maybe we should walk." Our building isn't that far away, about twenty minutes on foot. Usually I prefer to take the bus, since I'm always lugging around this heavy backpack. But on days like this, when it's absurdly late and overcrowded, it doesn't make much sense.

Obviously, Jason disagrees. "Nah, we got this."

The bus squeals to a halt fifteen feet short of the signpost. At once, the impatient herd of commuters swarms the front door before it even swings open. When it does, a crowd of people descends the steps, throwing elbows in an effort to reach the sidewalk. *F*-words are exchanged. Threats are leveled. I really want to walk home.

Jason takes my hand and pulls me away from the angry horde. "Come on," he says, leading me toward the exit at the back of the bus. When the last person hops down, Jason sticks his heel in the door to keep it from closing. Then he turns to me, and with a chivalrous sweep of his arm, says, "After you."

"Thanks." We're not supposed to enter through the back door because you pay up front, but we have free bus passes, so it doesn't really matter. The driver has bigger fish to fry right now, anyway.

"For the last time, this bus cannot move until everyone is behind the white line!" she yells. "If you cannot fit behind the white line, please exit and wait for the next bus."

For some reason, everyone's congregating in the middle of the bus, so it's actually pretty roomy back here. I step up, set my backpack at my feet, and hook my arm around a pole. Jason leans against the side of a seat and scrolls frantically through his phone. Probably deleting any incriminating evidence his parents might find while it's in their possession this weekend.

Finally, the bus hisses and lurches forward. We make our way slowly down the street.

Very slowly.

I recently read that New York City public buses are the slowest buses in the United States; in some neighborhoods, they travel at an average speed of five miles an hour. It's demeaning.

I'll be so happy to have a break from taking the bus this summer. The internship at ZigZag is residential, which means I'll get to spend six weeks living in Silicon Valley. No Brooklyn, no B9. I can't wait.

As I'm daydreaming about a new life on the West Coast, my

phone vibrates in my jacket pocket. At first, I assume it's a text from my mom—she always checks in with me before she leaves work—but it's actually an AirDrop. From a random stranger, presumably on this bus.

Your Secret Admirer
would like to
share a photo.

I tap the image to make it bigger. It's a cartoon drawing of a cat, eyes closed tightly, hugging a big pink heart. Above its head are the words HI, I THINK YOU'RE CUTE.

Someone on this bus thinks I'm cute?

Immediately and irrationally, I wonder if it's from Walker. Maybe he knows my name after all, and this secret crush I've been harboring since the end of sophomore year is, in fact, *not* unrequited. But the rational part of my brain reminds me this isn't possible. Before today, Walker has never acknowledged my existence, and besides that, he doesn't take the B9.

As discreetly as possible, I scan my surroundings, looking for someone who's looking at me. Practically everyone has their face buried in their phone, Jason included, except for a woman who's sleeping with her head against the window and a younger guy who's rapping along to the song streaming through his headphones. He abruptly stops to pull his phone from his pocket and frowns at whatever's on the screen. Then he nudges the girl next to him and shows it to her. She shrugs and shakes her head, then looks down at her own phone and lets out a little giggle.

Several phones ping at once. The normally quiet bus is suddenly filled with murmurs, a couple of airy laughs. Someone taps me on the shoulder. It's a man old enough to be my father, and he's smiling at me in a deeply creepy way.

"Did you send this to me?" he asks, holding his phone out so I can see. There's the cartoon cat hugging the heart, telling me he thinks I'm cute.

"I'm flattered," he says, as if this is a totally normal conversation to be having with a sixteen-year-old girl on a city bus. "But I'm married. If I were twenty years younger, though . . ."

Before he can say another word, I whirl away, sidling up next to Jason for cover. "Did you get this photo too?" I ask, but he's engrossed in his current task: covertly recording the crowd's reaction as they all realize they've received a mass AirDrop.

Dammit, Jason.

The bus brakes at the corner of Twenty-Third Avenue, and even though we still have one more stop to go, I shove my way out the back door.

"Ashley, wait!" Jason jumps off after me. "Where are you going?"

He's on my heels as I walk fast toward Bay Parkway. "I needed to get off that bus. Some creepy guy started talking to me after you sent that stupid photo." I pull up short and spin around, so suddenly we almost collide. "What is wrong with you?"

"Sorry. I thought it would be funny."

"Well, it wasn't. It was awkward and uncomfortable, and I'm sure I wasn't the only one who felt that way."

At least he has the courtesy to look sheepish. "I didn't think about that."

"You never think." I throw my hands up and start stalking down the street again.

"Ashley!" He runs to catch up with me and matches my

stride. "Ashley, I'm sorry. I just wanted to record some new content for my ZigZag channel."

"How much content could you possibly need? You spend too much time on these videos."

"Why? What else should I be doing?"

"You should do a legit extracurricular. It'll help you prep for college."

"Pssh. There's more important stuff than prepping for college."

"Like what?"

"Like having fun. We only get one run through high school, and we've gotta make the most of it. You're so caught up in perfecting your transcript, you don't ever make time to just enjoy yourself."

"I do so."

"Really? When's the last time you went on a date?"

Now it's my turn to squirm. I'm too embarrassed to admit I've never been on a date. I've never had a boyfriend. I've never even been kissed.

"I don't have to answer that," I say.

"Fine. But it's Friday, spring break has officially begun, and I'll bet you don't even have plans for tonight."

"You're right, I don't. But neither do you."

"What are you talking about? Of course I do." Then he winces, remembering the fact that he's grounded for those confetti-cannon shenanigans. "Oh, right."

"I repeat: was it worth it?"

"You won't be so smug once I'm rolling in that sweet ZigZag dough."

"Post a video that's *actually* funny and maybe you'll finally make some money off your channel."

His brown eyes glimmer. "Is that a challenge?"

I can't help but smile. "Maybe."

We walk down the path toward our apartment building, and he holds the front door open so I can enter first. In the elevator, he presses the buttons for our respective floors—four for him, five for me—and asks, "What time does your shift start tomorrow morning?"

"Ten." We both work at ShopRite on weekends.

"Me too. Wanna walk together?"

"I can't. I'm getting breakfast with my dad beforehand. I'll just meet you there."

"Okay." He fidgets with something in his jacket pocket, and just before the door retracts, he rubs his palm against the elevator wall. "Have a good night," he says, and he's gone.

As the door closes, I notice a sticker right where his palm was resting. It's big and official-looking, and says NOW VOICE-ACTIVATED: STATE YOUR FLOOR NUMBER LOUD AND CLEAR!

Another prank.

Jason Eisler will never change.

Chapter Four

When most non-Brooklynites think about Brooklyn, they probably envision this supercool place brimming with famous attractions and historic monuments: Coney Island, the Barclays Center, the Botanic Garden, the iconic bridge.

But I don't think they realize exactly how big Brooklyn is. I mean, it's really, really big. In terms of land, it's almost three times as big as Manhattan. More than two and a half million people live in at least sixty-six different neighborhoods, each of which has its own distinct style and personality.

I live in Mapleton, which is a small community in southwest Brooklyn, sandwiched among the bigger neighborhoods of Bensonhurst, Borough Park, and Midwood. There's nothing particularly notable about Mapleton; it's just your run-of-the-mill residential area. If I wanted to visit one of those famous attractions or historic monuments, I'd have to take the subway for at least a half hour, and most days, I never even get on the train.

So *my* Brooklyn isn't necessarily the supercool Brooklyn that most people envision, but it's the Brooklyn I call home.

I've lived in the same apartment my entire life. Well,

technically, not my *entire* life. For the first six months or so, I lived in some basement apartment in Bay Ridge. This was back when my parents were still together. Mom said the whole place smelled like mildew and the upstairs neighbors were always screaming. Thankfully, I don't remember anything about it.

I only remember living here, in apartment 5E.

Everything about this place is so familiar, I feel like the blueprints are etched in my brain. I don't have to think about which way to turn when I exit the elevator on the fifth floor, or how far to walk down the hallway, or even which keys to use for each of the three locks I need to open the front door. It's all done on autopilot. One minute I'm walking through the lobby, the next I'm in my room, backpack and jacket and sneakers in a heap at my feet.

This afternoon, though, my mind is still back in that elevator, chewing over Jason's words.

We only get one run through high school, and we've gotta make the most of it.

Well, isn't that precisely what I'm doing? Making the most of my high school career? Not by hanging out and screwing around, but by investing time, effort, and energy that will pay off later on. Jason acts like I'm wasting my teenage years, but I'm not. I'm preparing for the future. Because I firmly believe that if I work hard enough, the best is yet to come.

That's a phrase on my vision board: *The best is yet to come.* I put the board together earlier this year, when I really started getting serious about college prep. There's something inspirational about seeing all my hopes and dreams for the future gathered in one big collage. It reminds me there's a world out there beyond high school. Beyond Brooklyn, even.

My vision board is pretty simple, just something I threw

together with a photo-editing app. The logos for Stanford and Berkeley. Photos of tech campuses in Silicon Valley, like the Googleplex and, of course, ZigZag headquarters. Real-estate listings for homes in the Bay Area—especially ones with big backyards, because one day I'd really love to live in something bigger than this tiny apartment. And some inspirational quotes, like *The best is yet to come* and *Only you can control your future.*

It's tacked up on the wall above my desk, where I can see it every day. I'm staring at it when my phone dings with a text from Mom: *On my way home. Will you order a pizza?*

I respond with a thumbs-up emoji. Immediately, I dial up Vinnie's and order a large pie, half-pepperoni, with an order of garlic knots. My stomach starts to rumble at the thought of all that greasy delicious food.

In the meantime, I turn my attention back to my vision board, which suddenly looks incomplete. I have pictures of where I want to go to college, where I want to work, even where I want to live. But only now do I realize there's nothing on there about love or relationships. My future completely lacks romance.

Kind of like my present.

My phone buzzes. Probably Mom again with an update on her commute. The N train always gets delayed at rush hour. But when I pick up my phone, it's not a text message, but an email. From ZigZag.

Omigod. This is it.

My heart pounds and my palms start to sweat and I know I should probably treat this moment with the gravity it deserves, but I'm too anxious to do anything but squeal and jab at my phone until the body of the email fills my screen. And when it does, my heart pounds even faster. Except now the pounding isn't in my chest, but in the deepest pit of my stomach. Because this email doesn't say what it's supposed to say.

> Dear Applicant,
>
> Thank you for applying to the ZigZag summer internship program. This year, we had a record number of highly motivated applicants and a very limited number of spaces available in our program. Selecting a cohort is always a difficult decision, and after carefully reviewing your application, we've identified other candidates whose qualifications are more closely aligned with our program's eligibility requirements. Therefore, we are unable to offer you a

That's where I stop reading. I can't even process the rest of it. The phone slips out of my hand and onto the floor, and I sink down to the carpet beside it.

I didn't get into the summer program.

This can't be right. Did they confuse me with another person? The email was addressed "Dear Applicant," not "Dear Ms. Bergen," so it's entirely possible they meant to send it to someone else. Because this can't be happening. This can't be right.

Except it is. I feel the truth of it in the pit of my stomach, right where my heart is pounding, each frantic beat a reminder of my inadequacy. I didn't get in.

And I thought I was a shoo-in. Could I have been any farther off base?

The thing is, I'd given it my best shot. I worked hard, studied for hours, wrote the strongest personal statements I could. But my best wasn't good enough.

I can't help but wonder what went wrong, or why my qualifications aren't "closely aligned" with the requirements of the program. Was it that B I got in social studies last year? It's always been my weakest subject; that's why I decided to take regular American History instead of the harder AP course this year. Was that a mistake? All my other classes are AP or honors-level, though. Do they expect me to excel at everything?

This seems utterly hopeless.

Well, that's it. No summer internship in Silicon Valley for me. No big plans for this summer at all, actually. It's too late to apply for any other internships or immersion programs, since the deadlines have already passed. I should've applied to more than just one.

Guess I'll be spending my summer ringing up groceries at ShopRite. Great. That's exactly what the admissions officers at Stanford will want to see.

Then, a terrifying thought occurs to me: If I couldn't get into this competitive six-week summer program, what makes me think I'll be able to get into a school as prestigious and competitive as Stanford or Berkeley? What if all this nonstop work of preparing for college has been a big, fat waste of time?

Tears spring up from nowhere and suddenly my vision is blurry. When I look up, I can barely make out the words plastered on my vision board, though of course I know them by heart. I've seen them a million times. *The best is yet to come. Only you can control your future.*

What a crock.

I always thought I had control over my future, but it turns out, my future is completely out of my hands. It's controlled by a stranger in an office somewhere who decides my worth by comparing me to other strangers. Despite all my planning and struggling and strategizing, there's never been any guarantee of success.

This vision board is a joke. An embarrassment. Tangible evidence of how foolish I am. Or how foolish I was. Because now I know better.

In a flash, I rip my vision board down off the wall and tear it in half, then in quarters, then into pieces so small I can no longer fit them back together. All the while, I'm crying, tears dripping down my cheeks and onto the tiny scraps of paper. My dreams are now decimated and unrecognizable.

I can't stop crying; it's a force that has taken over my entire body. My chest heaves, my shoulders shake. I am so lost in my own despair that I don't even hear when the delivery guy arrives. It isn't until Mom appears at the threshold to my room, carrying a pizza box topped with a grease-stained paper bag, that I wipe my eyes and return to the present moment.

"Honey, what's going on? Why are you crying?" She sets the box on the floor and hurries to my side, purse still hanging on her shoulder. "Are you okay? Are you sick?"

"No," I say, suddenly feeling very guilty when I see the look of terror on her face. She's always worrying about me. There's a deep crease in her forehead and I'm sure I'm responsible for more than a few of those gray hairs that have sprouted up around her temple. "I'm fine, I just . . . I didn't get into the summer program at ZigZag."

Speaking the words out loud makes me start sobbing all over again. Mom hugs me close, rubbing my back in slow circles. But while her touch is a physical comfort, it does nothing to ease my sadness.

"This is the worst, Mom."

"I'm so sorry, sweetie."

"I wanted this so bad. I can't believe I didn't get in."

"Oh, I know you're disappointed, but I promise you there will be other amazing opportunities and . . . Wait, what's this?"

I open my eyes to see her staring at the shreds of paper scattered around the floor. Her eyes drift to the now-empty space above my desk, then back to me. "Oh, Ashley. Sweetie, this isn't the end of the road, it's just a minor setback. Rejections happen. You can't let them stop you from achieving your dreams."

By definition, this rejection has stopped me from achieving my dream. I'm not going to Silicon Valley this summer. Dream: squashed.

But I can't say that to Mom right now. Look at the way she's huddled up next to me, rubbing my back, the crease in her forehead twitching as she studies my face. She's trying her best to make me feel better.

"You're right," I say, though I don't believe it. "This is just a minor setback."

"You can do whatever you set your mind to. Don't let anyone make you feel differently." Mom wipes the tears from my cheeks and hugs me for a long moment. Then she says, "Come on. Let's eat before this pizza gets cold."

We spend the rest of the night in the living room, eating dinner in front of the TV. I chew and swallow my food, but I don't taste anything. I can't tell you what show we're watching, either. Because my entire worldview has been turned upside down.

I don't have control over my future.

And if I don't have control over my future, then maybe Jason's right. Maybe I'm not making the most of my one run through high school.

Maybe it's time to start having more fun.

Chapter Five

It's one thing to *say* I want to have more fun, but it's quite another to make it a reality. Thus far, I've devoted most of my high school career to the pursuit of a perfect transcript. That's serious business. I can't just go from zero to sixty overnight.

Which is why I'm all mopey at breakfast the next morning. Even though I should be celebrating the first official day of spring break, I'm still crushed about my rejection from Zig-Zag and not looking forward to a long day of stocking shelves and bagging groceries. Dad seems completely oblivious to my angst, though. He's all smiles as he orders his egg-white omelet from the server.

"I'll have that with spinach and feta, and sub a bialy for the toast, young lady."

He winks and laughs, as though he's said something funny, but the waitress (who is not particularly young) isn't amused. She scribbles the order on her pink notepad and turns to me. "For you, dear?"

"A Belgian waffle with strawberries, please."

"Whipped cream?" Her voice is hoarse, like Ms. Henley's.

"Yes, please."

"You got it." She takes our menus and heads back to the counter.

My dad and I have never had the kind of relationship where we talk about feelings. I'm assuming he has them, but he's never shared them with me, nor has he ever asked me about mine. Never a "How are you feeling, Ashley?" or an "Are you doing okay?" It used to bother me, because Mom is exactly the opposite—she can't *stop* talking about feelings—but I've learned to live with it by now.

So I can't say I'm surprised that he hasn't asked me what's wrong, despite the fact that I'm slouched over and sighing every five seconds. Instead, he stirs cream into his coffee and starts talking about Stefanie.

"Stefanie's going to the spa with her girlfriends today, so I've gotta take the boys to soccer practice this afternoon."

Stefanie is my dad's wife. I refuse to call her my stepmother because in the three years they've been married, she's never acted remotely maternal toward me. "The boys" are her tween sons, Axel and Milo. I barely know them at all, but apparently, Dad knows all about their soccer schedules. Which is interesting, considering he never has time to attend any of my awards ceremonies or science fairs. I wonder if he ever talks to *them* about feelings.

When Dad and Stefanie first moved in together, I used to spend weekends at their house on Long Island. It's enormous and picture-perfect, with a big backyard. Kind of like some of the houses I had on my vision board. Anyway, I haven't been there in almost a year, because I'm not exactly welcome there.

To be fair, they've never told me I'm not welcome there. But I've never *felt* welcome. I'm always doing or saying the wrong thing. The last time I went, Stefanie threw a fit because I didn't use a coaster on the coffee table. She shrieked, "Are you insane? This is Peruvian walnut wood!" before pulling on a pair of rubber gloves and attacking the nonexistent watermark with a massive bottle of furniture polish.

Five minutes later, Dad was driving me home. He didn't say a word the entire ride back to Brooklyn. He didn't ask me if I was okay or apologize for what happened. When Mom asked me why I came home early, I lied and told her I had to finish writing an English paper.

The truth is, I just didn't want Mom and Dad to get in another fight, and I knew this would cause one. My entire childhood was riddled with memories of the two of them fighting, sometimes about big things, sometimes about things that didn't matter at all. It got worse once he started dating Stefanie, and I was over it. So rather than continue to feel uncomfortable at Dad's house or be forced to explain to Mom why I didn't want to go there, I got a job at ShopRite, with regular shifts on Saturdays and Sundays.

Working in Brooklyn has been a really convenient excuse to avoid going to Long Island on the weekends. Instead, Dad dips into Mapleton for breakfast or lunch or the occasional dinner. At first, he came every weekend, then every other weekend, and now it's more like once a month. It's hard for him to get out of Long Island, he says. He's got his hands full with his family. The boys' soccer games and everything. There's always some last-minute excuse.

At least I don't have to see Stefanie anymore.

Unfortunately, I still have to hear about her. Dad's been talking about her nonstop for the past ten minutes. "Stefanie booked us a trip to Club Med. Got a last-minute deal on one of those travel websites. It's a nice family-friendly resort down in the Bahamas. We're leaving next weekend. The boys are really looking forward to it."

I guess I'm not getting an invite. Not that I want to spend a week trapped on an island with Stefanie, getting yelled at for using the wrong fork at dinner or something, but it would've been nice to have been included. To have Dad acknowledge that I'm his daughter, and therefore a part of his family. Even if Stefanie won't acknowledge it.

When the waitress delivers our breakfast, Dad finally stops talking about Stefanie. He slices into his omelet with the side of his fork and finally asks, "How's school?"

"Fine."

"Staying out of trouble?"

"Yes."

"Still getting straight As?"

I nod and shovel a forkful of warm, whipped-cream-smothered waffle into my face. No need to mention that B I got in social studies.

"You've always been smart," he says.

"Not smart enough for ZigZag," I say.

"What do you mean?"

"I didn't get into their summer internship program."

"What's that?"

He can't be serious. I wait for him to tell me his question is a joke, even though it would be the worst, most insensitive joke in the history of father-daughter relationships. But from the way his brows are pinched together, it's clear he's legitimately clueless.

I've been talking about this program nonstop since I first found out about it back in October. That was five months ago, which means I've seen Dad at least five times since then, and I'm absolutely certain I've told him about it. Is he not listening when I speak, or does he just not care enough to remember anything I say?

"It's a six-week summer internship program," I say. "It takes place at their headquarters in Silicon Valley."

"Oh, that sounds great."

"I know." *Thanks for rubbing it in, Dad.* "But they didn't accept me."

He makes this dismissive sound, halfway between a sigh and a grunt, then shrugs his shoulders. "You know how these things work."

"Yeah. My grades weren't good enough." Or maybe it was my personal essay that sucked. Or maybe my extracurriculars weren't impressive. Whatever it was that sealed my fate: "*I wasn't good enough.*"

"Look, Ashley, you're smart, but smarts only get you so far in this life. It's never what you know, it's who you know. Everything is about having the right connections. They probably handed out spots to the kids of the people who work there. Or else someone was greasing their pockets. Look at what happened at USC with the lady from *Full House.*"

I stab a strawberry slice with my fork. "I really thought I was gonna get in."

"Yeah, well, life doesn't always go according to plan." His tone is clipped, like he's annoyed at me for being so upset.

His phone starts ringing. Loudly, because he always keeps the volume set to the absolute max. He pulls it from his pocket and looks at the screen, then swipes to answer and starts talking. Loudly, because he doesn't appear to realize we're in a diner full of people.

"Okay, sugar," he says. "Of course, honey, no problem."

Obviously, it's Stefanie.

He never takes a clipped tone with her. Of course he doesn't, she's his meal ticket. Dad's living proof of the fact that people don't get ahead because of their skills or their talent or their excellent high school transcripts, but because they have the right connections. He didn't even go to college, and now he's living it up in his beautiful home, a quick ten-minute trip to the beach, which he can easily drive to in one of his two gleaming SUVs. And it's all because he married a rich woman.

Meanwhile, my mom has gotten absolutely nowhere with her college degree. She works a forty-hour week at a job she hates. Her paycheck barely covers our expenses on our run-down rental apartment, which hasn't had a fresh coat of paint in years. She doesn't have a car, not even a beater. So what was the point of all that hard work?

Maybe I should spend less time studying and more time making the right connections. Or at least trying to score a date.

A moment later, he ends the call and puts the phone back in his pocket. "That was Stefanie." *Duh.*

He tears into his bialy, crumbs and bits of onion falling to his plate. Not for the first time, I wonder if this man is actually my father. Maybe my real father is someone else, someone who cares about the way I'm feeling. Maybe he works at ZigZag. If so, he could probably help me get into the summer program. At the very least, he'd know what the summer program is.

Dad's already talking about something else. What little appetite I had is long gone, so I push the strawberry slices around on my plate just to give myself something to do.

The hostess passes our table, menus in hand, with two men following closely behind. One of them is wearing cologne, and it smells so good, like one of those clove-studded oranges. The way Walker smelled in class yesterday.

I watch as they take their seats in a booth diagonally across from ours. The man with his back to me is older, around Dad's age. But the other man isn't a man at all; he's a teenager, and when he turns around to sit down, I actually gasp.

Omigod.

It's Walker Beech.

Dad's voice fades into background noise. In fact, the whole diner seems to fall away. All I can see is Walker, the most beautiful person in the room. Possibly in the entire borough of Brooklyn.

His hair is still perfectly tousled, which makes me think it's a natural phenomenon, because the rest of him looks like he just rolled out of bed. There's even a crease on his face from where the pillow undoubtedly hugged his cheek all night. Though he did take the time to apply that incredible-smelling cologne, so maybe he made time to style his hair, too.

He opens his menu with those impeccable hands, fingertips playing with the laminated corners, while his hazel eyes scan the pages for his perfect meal. I wonder if he prefers sweet or savory breakfasts. Maybe he likes a little bit of each, like challah French toast with a side of bacon.

A moment later, he slaps the menu closed and lays it flat on the table, resting his clasped hands on top of it. Then he unclasps them and starts tapping out an irregular rhythm with his fingertips. All the while, he's staring at the guy across the table from him, who I'm assuming is his dad, though I can only see him from behind. His hair is thin and cropped short, but it's curly, just like Walker's.

My gaze drifts back to Walker's hands, which are now ripping the edges of his napkin to shreds. Suddenly, he stops, and when I look up at his face, he's looking at me.

I've been caught staring. Again.

There's something like recognition in his eyes. I mean, it's been less than twenty-four hours since he plucked that confetti from my hair. We shared a moment. He must remember my face.

Before I can confirm or reject my hypothesis, the waitress approaches his table and blocks him from view.

I breathe out, my veins flooding with a mixture of relief and terror. Relief because now I have a moment of reprieve. Terror because I know that moment is fleeting. Dad's blissfully eating his omelet, having a one-sided conversation with himself, while I'm trying not to panic. I smooth my hands over my hair, tucking it behind my ears, then untucking it and letting it hang free to frame my face. Why didn't I think to put on lip gloss this morning? Or wear something nicer than this ratty Murrow sweatshirt?

The waitress steps away and there's Walker again, staring at his dad with this serious look on his face. He's sitting on his hands now, the way you do when you're nervous and trying not to fidget.

It's always weird running into someone outside of the places where you usually see them. Up until now, I've only ever seen Walker at school. Walking in the hallways or sitting in class or lined up in the lunchroom.

So it could just be the unusual setting, but he seems a little off. Normally, he exudes this effortless cool, like nothing ever fazes him. Right now, though, he definitely seems fazed. And his dad is making these big, sweeping hand motions as he talks. Whatever he's saying must be important. Unlike whatever my dad is talking about now.

When his dad pauses his speech to take a long sip of water, Walker looks down, then over at me. This time, I don't panic or freeze, and I don't avert my gaze. Instead, I smile. Just a little. Just so he knows I see him.

I hold my breath, suddenly full of regret for being so bold. What made me think Walker would remember my face? The confetti moment, it was significant to me. But to him, it probably meant nothing.

Then something miraculous happens: Walker smiles back at me. His lips part slightly and his hazel eyes shine and I'm pretty sure time stands completely still. My brain whispers telepathic messages across the crowded diner: *Hey there. You look great today. Actually, you always look great.*

"Do you think this is funny?"

A sharp, stern voice ruins the magic. Time shoots into forward motion again and Walker quickly looks away, toward his dad, who gestures angrily as he issues reprimands and a few choice insults.

Walker's whole body turns inward. He crosses his arms against his chest, ducks his chin, lowers his gaze. His knee is bouncing up and down and I want nothing more than to reach out and steady it.

Then, in an instant, he's on his feet, striding toward the exit. He avoids my gaze as he passes me by, leaving a trail of cologne in his wake. I turn to see him push open the front door and march out onto the sidewalk. His dad's still sitting in their booth, eating his eggs. It doesn't look like he plans to go after him.

Meanwhile, my dad's completely oblivious to what just happened. He's still yammering on about Stefanie. He might as well be talking to himself.

What am I even doing here? What purpose do these stupid sporadic breakfasts serve, for either of us? Dad doesn't care about me. He doesn't want to be here. And the truth is, neither do I.

I want to be out on Kings Highway, running after Walker. I want to grab his hand and say that I'm sorry for getting him in trouble and tell him how great he looks today and every other day.

I may not have control over my future, but I do have control over this moment. I can choose to sit here and be miserable. Or I can choose to stand up and follow my heart.

In a flash, I crumple my napkin and toss it onto my plate. "I've gotta go, Dad."

"But you haven't finished your waffle." He looks completely perplexed at this last-minute change of plans.

"I'm not hungry." I slip out of the booth and give him a quick kiss on the cheek. "I've gotta get to work."

"Don't you need a ride?" He calls after me, but I'm already out the door, flying down the steps and onto the sidewalk, hoping Walker hasn't gone too far.

Chapter Six

I spot Walker two blocks up, just before he turns right onto East Seventh Street. Instantly, I break into a run, the soles of my Converse slapping against the uneven pavement. There's an urgency to each step, like if I don't catch up to him now, I'll lose him forever.

By the time I finally reach him, I'm completely out of breath. He flinches when I touch his arm, and he pulls away from my grasp with a jolt. Then he spins around and looks at me, his brows knotted together. "What're you doing here?"

This was probably a bad idea. Walker must think I'm a weirdo.

Still, I've come this far and there's no undoing it now. I've gotta say something. So even though I'm panting and sweaty and tongue-tied, I manage to squeak out a "Hi."

The corner of his mouth quirks up. "Hi."

He definitely thinks I'm a weirdo.

I clear my throat and continue. "I just wanted to say I'm sorry."

"For what?"

"For what happened back there in the diner. I didn't mean to get you in trouble."

He shakes his head. "You don't have to apologize. You didn't get me in trouble. Trust me, I was already in trouble with my dad."

He doesn't elaborate and I don't ask him to. Instead, I try to make him laugh. "If it's any consolation, I was having a pretty miserable time in there with my father, too. Maybe it's a holiday we don't know about? National Hate on Your Kids During Breakfast Day?"

My plan works. He lets out a little chuckle and says, "I'm kinda regretting running out like that, though. Now I'm hungry and I didn't get to eat my food."

"Wanna go back? I'll walk in with you and we can pretend like nothing ever happened."

"Nah, I can't deal with my dad. He'll be extra mad now. But thanks for the offer."

"Anytime."

There's an awkward pause and the sounds around us seem to amplify. Birds chirp in the tree across the street. Horns blare on Kings Highway.

Walker shoves his hands in the pockets of his jeans and asks, "Where are you headed?"

What I want to say is, "Wherever you're going." But my shift starts in twenty minutes, so instead I say, "I've gotta go to work."

"Where do you work?"

"ShopRite. The one on Avenue I."

"That's kind of a long walk from here."

"Yeah, it is." Maybe I shouldn't have ditched out on that ride from my dad. I'm going to clock in late for the first time ever.

"I'll walk with you," he says, "if you want."

On second thought, a long walk sounds absolutely perfect.

As we start down the street, everything suddenly seems different. Technically, spring started days ago, on the vernal equinox. But it didn't *feel* like spring started until this very moment. The air is fresh and full of promise. The sky is a bright, cloudless blue. It's the first day of spring break and Walker Beech is strolling beside me. It's truly the dawn of a whole new season.

"So, what was your dad giving you shit about?" he asks.

"He wasn't giving me shit." He never does, really. I'm pretty sure he doesn't care enough about who I am or what I do to give me shit.

"Then why were you having a miserable time?"

"Because I'm always miserable when I'm with my father."

"I know what you mean," Walker says. "Do you ever feel like your parents don't like you?"

"Yes. Not my mom, but my dad. Although, it's less that he doesn't like me and more that he kind of wishes I didn't exist. Maybe that's the same thing, I don't know." I stare straight ahead at the long stretch of sidewalk, realizing this is the first time I've ever acknowledged my father's apathy toward me out loud. It stings a little.

"Well," he says, "my dad was definitely giving me shit back there."

"About what?"

"My grades. Again. It's always about my grades."

I bite my bottom lip to hide my surprise. I never would've suspected Walker got bad grades. Granted, I don't know him well—or at all, really—but he always seems so attentive in

Ms. Henley's class. Always taking notes and looking at the whiteboard.

That is, when he's not secretly texting.

"Grades aren't everything," I say. A total platitude, to be sure, but I don't know how else to respond.

He grimaces. "Tell that to my dad. I failed my algebra midterm and he's acting like I ruined my whole life. It's like he wants me to be someone I'm not. Someone smart."

"Just because you're failing algebra, it doesn't mean you're not smart. Who's your teacher?"

"Franzen."

"Well, that explains it. Franzen sucks."

I had Mr. Franzen for Algebra II and he did indeed suck. Algebra II is a class for juniors, which is why Walker is taking it now. But I'm in the accelerated math program, which means I took it when I was a sophomore. This year, I'm in pre-calculus with Mr. Kiernan, a teacher who's much, *much* better than Mr. Franzen.

"Did you fail his class too?"

"No." Actually, I got an A, but I'm not about to rub that in Walker's face. "His lectures were terrible, though. He was always going off on tangents about what it was like growing up in Brooklyn in the 1980s, how he went to school with one of the Beastie Boys. Like anyone cared."

"I know, right? Just teach me how to solve for x and shut up."

We burst out laughing as we cross the street. I'm amazed at how natural it feels to be hanging out with Walker, how easily the conversation flows. Turns out there was nothing to be nervous about.

"Anyway," he says, "Franzen told me I can bring my grade

up if I do this online extra credit assignment over spring break. There's, like, a hundred questions, and I have no idea what I'm doing. This morning, I was trying to tell my dad that I can't figure it out, but he said I was being lazy and stupid." He scowls and sucks his teeth. "I'd like to see him answer these questions. It's not like he's so brilliant."

He turns inward again, digging his hands deeper into his pockets and pressing his lips into a tight, thin line. There's pain in his eyes. It makes me realize that my relationship with my dad isn't all that bad. He may not care about who I am or what I do, but at least he doesn't tell me I'm stupid.

There's nothing I can do to change the way his father sees him, but maybe I can change the way Walker sees himself.

"Let me help you with your extra credit," I say. "I took Algebra II last year, so I know it really well."

His eyes light up. "You wanna do the assignment for me?"

"No, no. I can't do it for you, but I can help you figure it out. I'm on the peer tutoring team. I've done stuff like this before. We can work through the problems together. Slowly, so you can understand them."

He looks skeptical. "Thanks for the offer, but it's due the Monday we go back to school. You can't waste your whole spring break teaching me how to do math."

"It won't take the whole break. It'll probably only take a couple of afternoons. Besides, it's not a waste. I'd be happy to do it."

He smiles at me, the same beautiful smile he gave me back in the diner. "Thanks. That's really sweet of you."

My insides melt like butter in a frying pan. Running out on my dad was the best choice I've made this year. Possibly the best choice I've made in my entire life.

"What else do you have planned for the break?" he asks. "You know, aside from saving my ass from failing algebra."

"The thing I'm looking forward to the most is the hackathon."

"Hackathon?" He lowers his voice and says, "Are you hacking into computers or something?"

"Uh . . ." I laugh uncomfortably. "No. I'm not, like, doing anything illegal. A hackathon is basically just a coding marathon."

"Oh." He seems disappointed.

"Other than that, I'll be hanging around, working at Shop-Rite, hoping to run into Taylor Swift." He eyes me suspiciously until I tell him, "She's got a concert at Barclays Center next week, so she'll be in Brooklyn at some point. Obviously, I don't really think I'm going to run into her. It was a joke. I'm a huge Taylor Swift fan."

"Are you going?" he asks. "To the concert?"

"Nah, tickets are super expensive. It sucks, but I'll just have to wait for the Netflix special. What about you? What are your plans for spring break?"

He shrugs. "Nothing. Just hanging around."

We walk in silence for a few seconds before he says, "Wanna hang around together? I mean, besides working on the extra credit assignment. No math. No work. Just . . . fun."

Is this what I think it is? No, it can't be.

But there's no other explanation.

I am almost one hundred percent certain that Walker Beech is asking me on a date.

My very *first* date.

A dozen confetti cannons explode in my chest. There are streamers and glitter and sequins, a sparkling rainbow swirling around. It's a beautiful, fluttery mess, so big and so dense that it crowds out the air in my lungs. I can hardly breathe.

My answer comes out as a whisper. "Sure."

"Cool." He casually whips out his phone to save my number to his contacts. It's a strain to keep my voice steady as I recite each digit.

The remainder of our walk is a blur, coming into focus only as we approach the entrance to ShopRite. On the far end of the parking lot, Jason is already hard at work, gathering shopping carts from the return stalls. I don't even want to know how late I am.

"This is me," I say, pointing to the store. "Thanks for keeping me company."

"No problem. I'll text you later."

We say goodbye and I stand there, watching him walk away until he disappears onto McDonald Avenue. Then I hurry toward the automatic sliding doors, prepared to apologize to my boss for being late. I'm sure he'll understand. It's not like I've ever done this before.

I'm about to cross the threshold when a shopping cart juts into my path, blocking my way. Jason's behind it, scowling.

"Since when are you friends with Walker Beech?" His tone is unusually pissy.

"What's your problem?"

"You said you were getting a ride from your dad this morning. Why'd you lie to me?"

"I didn't lie. There was a last-minute change of plans."

I try to shimmy around the shopping cart, but Jason angles it so I can't pass by. "You had breakfast with him?"

"What difference does it make?"

"He's a jerk, Ashley."

"He's not a jerk." I shove the shopping cart with so much force it goes careening back into the parking lot. Jason grabs it a split second before it bumps into a car that's illegally parked at the curb.

I stalk into the store and hang a left into the staff room. My boss is nowhere to be seen. As I'm slipping my red ShopRite vest over my sweatshirt, Jason walks through the door with a sheepish look on his face. "I'm sorry," he says. "Just be careful with him. That's all I'm saying."

"Don't worry about me, I'll be fine." I shove my bag into my locker and whirl around. "Yesterday, you were giving me a hard time about how I never go on any dates or have any fun. So why are you judging me for it now?"

His mouth falls open. "Wait, you guys were on a date?"

I brush past him without answering. I have to admit, it's funny to see him looking so shocked. Because it's sort of a shocking revelation. Me, on a date with Walker Beech. Who would've thought?

But spring has sprung. And it's the dawn of a whole new Ashley.

Chapter Seven

The old Ashley would've been fine with going home after work and spending yet another Saturday night alone in her bedroom. The new Ashley? She wants to go out tonight and have a little fun.

Heaven doesn't leave for Puerto Rico until next weekend, and I really want to see my best friends. As soon as my shift ends, I text Heaven and Christine.

Let's do something tonite!

Christine:
YESSS. What do you wanna do?

Idk. I just don't wanna stay home.

Heaven:
We could go to Sheepshead Bay.
Maybe Roll N Roaster?
I'm in the mood for a roast beef sandwich.

I know what Heaven's in the mood for, and it's not a roast beef sandwich. Though Roll-N-Roaster does have good food—yummy meats, cottage fries, and "cheez on anything you pleez"—she really wants to go there to ogle Shawn Booker, a senior at Murrow who works behind the counter. She's had a crush on him forever.

The thought of cheez fries makes my mouth water and Christine says her dad can drive us there, so just like that, my Saturday night's booked.

When I tell Mom about my dinner plans, she looks pleasantly surprised. "That's great, sweetie," she says. "I'm glad you're going out with the girls. Just be home by ten, okay?"

My curfew is earlier than anyone else's I know. Christine's is midnight, Heaven's is one o'clock. I'm not sure Jason even has a curfew—when he's not grounded, that is. It's not like I want to stay out super late tonight or anything, but it would be nice to have the option. I get good grades and stay out of trouble. What more do I have to do to prove to my mom that I deserve some more freedom?

I don't feel like fighting with her, though, so I just say "Okay."

When we get to Roll-N-Roaster, the line stretches halfway across the huge dining room. We stand at the back of it and Heaven cranes her neck above the crowd to check out the situation at the registers.

"Is Shawn working tonight?" I ask.

"I'm not sure." Heaven shrugs, trying to evoke a sense of indifference and failing miserably.

"He's right there." Christine points to the kiosk on the far right, where Shawn is standing beneath a big yellow sign that reads ORDER HERE PLEEZ!

"Don't point!" Heaven swats at Christine's hand, then fluffs out her hair. "How do I look?"

"Fabulous," I say. "As usual."

"Are you actually going to talk to him this time?" Christine says.

Heaven takes a deep breath and holds it for a second, contemplating her response. We've been here three times in the past month. Each time, Shawn was our cashier. Each time, Heaven swore she was going to talk to him. And each time, Heaven completely chickened out.

It's weird. She's probably the most confident girl I know, always laughing in the face of a challenge and letting insults roll right off her back. But whenever Shawn's around, she turns into this meek, nervous person who can't string two words together.

A crush is a powerful thing.

Considering what happened with *my* crush this morning, I'm inspired to give her a pep talk. "You have to talk to him, okay? You can do it. Don't be afraid."

She huffs out a breath. "What should I say to him?"

"Start with hi." That's how I started my conversation with Walker. And look how well that worked out!

"Right." She nods, looking thoroughly unconvinced.

As we creep closer to the front of the line, I study the huge, backlit menu posted above the registers. I always get the same thing when we come here: turkey sandwich, cheez fries, and a lemonade. Maybe I'll switch things up a little tonight. A strawberry shake sounds good.

Before I know it, we're up. Shawn calls "Next!" and waves us over to the counter. Heaven doesn't budge, so Christine and I give her a little shove forward.

"Welcome to Roll-N-Roaster," he says. "May I take your order?"

Heaven is still frozen. I poke her in the ribs, and she squeaks out a minuscule "Hi."

"Uh . . . hi." We stand there for a few beats of awkward silence, Heaven wearing this painful grin, Christine visibly suppressing an eye roll. Shawn is understandably confused. "Are you guys ordering anything, or . . . ?"

Perhaps I should've given a better pep talk.

"I'll have a turkey sandwich and fries, both with cheez," I say.

"I'll have a roast beef with cheez, a side of onion rings, and a lemonade," Christine says.

Heaven's already run off toward the condiment bar without placing her order, so I add, "Make that two roast beefs with cheez. And a strawberry shake."

We catch up with her at a booth in the far corner of the dining room, where she's eating pickle slices at an alarming rate. The moment Christine opens her mouth to speak, Heaven cuts her off. "Don't even say it."

"I just don't understand why—"

"I said, don't say it."

"—you're so intimidated by him. He's cute and everything, but come on. You're the Queen, remember?"

Heaven sighs and picks at the edge of her kaiser roll. "I can't explain it."

"I understand completely," I say, because I know exactly what it's like to have a crush on a guy who makes you tongue-tied.

"You're both ridiculous." Christine shakes her head and sips her lemonade. Of course *she* doesn't understand. She thinks high school boys are immature; she's always talking about how she can't wait to go to college so she can finally meet some "men." I suspect college guys aren't much more sophisticated than their high school counterparts, but I don't want to ruin her fantasy.

"Can we talk about something else, please?" Heaven's cheeks are going pink.

"Fine," Christine says. "What'd you guys do today?"

Now's probably not the time to mention my act of courage in chasing down Walker this morning. It'll only make Heaven feel worse about chickening out yet again. Instead, I say, "Not much, just went to work. You?"

"Finished my wearable. The pendant changes color based on the temperature now."

"I worked on my tiara too," Heaven adds. "Almost got the voice control down."

"That's awesome. I really need to fix my hoodie. I haven't even touched it since yesterday afternoon."

I've got a lot of work to do on it, too. The LEDs may be lined up perfectly, but now I can't get them to blink. I have a sneaking suspicion my circuit isn't complete, which means I'll have to pick out the stitches—*again*—to see where I went wrong. It's beyond frustrating, especially since the girls have made so much progress on their projects. I don't like being left behind. Tomorrow, when I get home from work, I think I'll hunker down and focus on finishing it up.

"Oh, I got an email from Yale, too," Christine says. "They sent me a course selection guide for the summer study. There's a full-stack web development class that looks really good."

"Jealous," says Heaven.

"Why? You've got your job shadow. That's gonna be so cool."

"Yeah, but I'm still living in Brooklyn all summer. I wish I was going away, like you guys."

"I'm not going anywhere," I say, staring into my tray of crispy, golden cheez fries. Suddenly, they don't look so appetizing.

"What are you talking about?"

I lift my gaze and meet their eyes. "I'm not going to Silicon Valley. ZigZag rejected me."

Christine gasps. "No way."

"Are you sure?" Heaven asks, like maybe I read the email wrong.

"Yeah, I'm sure. They said my qualifications weren't 'closely aligned' with their requirements. So I'll be stuck in Brooklyn all summer, too."

"Ashley, I'm so sorry."

"When did you find out?"

"Last night." I shrug one shoulder. "Wasn't meant to be, I guess."

"There's gotta be some internships that are still accepting applications," Christine says.

"Maybe you can get a last-minute job shadow or something," offers Heaven.

"Probably not. It's almost April." I take a long pull on my strawberry shake and let the ice cream melt over my tongue. "It's fine, really. No big deal. I'll just get a whole lot more shifts at ShopRite. It'll be nice to earn some extra cash."

"You're taking this really well," Christine says. "I thought you'd be, like, devastated."

"What's the point in being upset about it? It's not like I ever had an actual chance of getting in."

"Of course you did. Your transcript is flawless, your SAT scores are amazing. You're basically a genius."

"None of that matters," I say, thinking back to breakfast with my dad. "Everything's about having the right connections. They probably only hand out spots in programs like this to people whose parents paid bribes or something."

Heaven scowls. "That's not true. You think someone paid a bribe for me to get my job shadow? Or for Christine to get into Yale?"

"No, no." Clearly, I hadn't thought through my father's philosophy. "What I mean is, there are so many factors that are out of my control. I have all these big dreams about where I want to go to college and what kind of job I want to have, but no matter how much I work or how hard I study, there's no guarantee I'll actually achieve them. The future's completely out of my hands."

"It's not *completely* out of your hands," Christine says.

"No, but I feel like maybe I should shift my priorities or something."

"What does that mean?"

"I want to start having more fun."

Christine and Heaven exchange a glance. "Are we not fun enough for you now?"

"No, you're loads of fun. I love you guys. But when was the last time any of us went on a date?"

Heaven snickers. "Talk about factors that are out of your control."

"Is it, though?" I glance over my shoulder, toward the register where Shawn is busy taking orders. "You could've said something back there, but you didn't."

Her cheeks flush and she takes a big bite of her sandwich. Christine chimes in with, "You know how I feel about high school boys."

"You've never even given them a chance. How do you know there isn't some super fantastic and totally mature eleventh grader out there, just waiting to bask in your magnificence?"

She laughs. "Why are you suddenly so obsessed with dating?"

I can barely restrain my ear-to-ear smile. "Because I have a date."

"With who?"

"Walker Beech."

Heaven clasps her hands to her mouth and lets out a squeal of joy. Christine looks less than impressed. "So, you're done planning for your future because some boy asked you out on a date?"

"That's not what I'm saying. But life doesn't have to be all work and no romance. I can be a good student *and* go out on dates. We only get one run through high school, after all. We have to make the most of it."

"Did you read that on some cheesy inspirational meme?"

"Ignore her," Heaven says, waving a dismissive hand in Christine's direction. "Tell me how this happened."

I take another long sip of my strawberry shake and relay the story of my morning. How I saw Walker across the crowded diner and followed him out the door. How we shared stories about our crappy dads and how I offered to help with his extra credit assignment. How he took my number and asked if I wanted to hang out together over spring break. My heart flutters as I relive each romantic detail.

"Wow." Heaven has her chin on her fist and her eyes are glistening. "That is amazing."

"When are you guys going out?" Christine asks.

"I'm not sure yet. We haven't made solid plans." I try to say this casually, but there's a small part of me that's in panic mode, worried that Walker didn't actually mean what he said about hanging out together. He hasn't texted me to follow up or anything.

"I'm super excited for you," Heaven says. "You're an inspiration, chasing after him like that."

Her gaze drifts over my shoulder and the dreamy smile on her face instantly melts to a look of sheer terror. "Omigod," she whispers.

I turn to see Shawn headed our way with a bus tub tucked under his arm. Two seconds later, he's standing over our table. "Can I clear your plates, or are you still eating?"

Christine pops the last of her sandwich into her mouth and I toss my napkin onto my empty tray. Heaven doesn't move; she's wearing that painful grin, again. I can't stand to see her squander another chance to talk to Shawn.

I squeeze her leg gently under the table. With a shaky voice, she says, "Yeah, you can take them. Thanks."

He smiles politely, then begins clearing away our dishes and silverware. Heaven looks my way and I mouth, "Don't be afraid."

She takes a deep breath and asks, "How's your spring break going, Shawn?"

"I feel like I haven't had much of a break yet," he says. "Worked last night, worked tonight. I've been busy."

"Well, you better make time for some fun." Her voice is stronger now. The confident Heaven is finally showing her face. "Priorities, Shawn."

His smile morphs from cool and polite to warm and friendly. "Yeah, you're right. What're you doing for fun?"

"You know." She gestures to me and Christine. "Just hanging around."

"Cool." He hoists his bus tub up on his shoulder. "Maybe I'll catch you hanging around, then."

As he walks away, Heaven mutters, "Omigod, omigod, omigod."

"That was amazing," I say.

"It was, wasn't it?" She tosses her curls over her shoulder, all trace of self-doubt gone. "I don't know what I was so afraid of."

"That's what I've been telling you all along," Christine says.

On the ride home, Christine's dad lets her commandeer the radio, so she puts on Taylor Swift's *1989*. As the opening notes to "Welcome to New York" pulse from the speakers, I sit silently in the backseat, staring out the window at the streets of Sheepshead Bay passing us by. Taylor definitely isn't singing about *this* New York in the song. She means Manhattan, of course, or maybe even downtown Brooklyn, where the lights are brighter and the buildings are taller and the possibilities for your life are seemingly endless.

By nine o'clock, I'm already in my pajamas and ready for bed. Another wild and crazy Saturday night for me.

I wonder what Walker's doing right now.

As I'm scrolling through Netflix to find the perfect distraction from my boring reality, my phone dings with a text. It's from Walker. Like he heard my thoughts or something.

wut r u up to tmrw?

Working until 4.
Then nothing.

not nothin
ur hangin w me 😉

I bury my face in my pillow and scream. Walker meant what he said. He actually wants to hang out together.

I'm going on my very first date!

Chapter Eight

The next day, work is a blur. My body may be bagging groceries and stocking shelves and mopping floors, but my mind is a million miles away, dreaming about my date with Walker. I'm meeting him tonight at six o'clock at Spumoni Gardens, a pizzeria in Bensonhurst. Then . . . who knows where the evening will take us?

I get home from work at four, which should give me just enough time to get ready. When I walk through the door, Mom asks what I want for dinner. "We've got pasta and sausage. I could throw together a—"

"Oh. I'm going out for dinner tonight. Didn't I tell you?"

"No, you didn't." There's a hint of disappointment in her voice. "Going out with the girls again?"

"Actually, I'm going out with this guy. Walker."

Her eyes narrow to slits. "Walker who?"

"Walker Beech."

She crosses her arms against her chest and glares at me. Mom is definitely not happy about this. She's always made it clear that she wants to meet any guy I go on a date with. So far, this has been a nonissue, since I've never gone out on a date. But I can't ask Walker to come pick me up just so Mom can grill him. I don't even know where he lives. Maybe our apartment building is totally out of his way.

I can sense she's about to protest, so I quickly say, "It's not a date or anything. I'm tutoring him in algebra. He's got this extra credit packet I'm helping him with and it's due the day we get back from spring break. We're gonna work on it while we eat."

It's not *really* a lie. It's more of a half-truth. Mom doesn't look totally thrilled with the idea, but she concedes. "Fine. But I want you to keep your phone location enabled. Do not turn it off for any reason."

That's another thing. Not only do I have the earliest curfew in the entire borough of Brooklyn, but my mom also insists on tracking my every move virtually whenever I'm out of the house. I'm not sure if she thinks I'm lying to her about where I'm going, or if she's worried Walker's going to abduct me. Either way, it's an easy request to comply with. I always keep my location on anyway.

After taking a shower, I spend way too long choosing an outfit. Every piece of clothing I own is in a pile on the floor as I work to choose the perfect look. After testing several contenders, I settle on a cream-colored loose sweater with a pink cami underneath, a flowery pink scarf, skinny black jeans, and my Converse.

Then I throw my hair into what I hope is a stylish ponytail, slick on a coat of lip gloss, and clasp my favorite necklace around my neck—a long chain with a pendant shaped like a paper airplane. It's just like the one Taylor Swift sings about in "Out of the Woods," the necklace she supposedly got from Harry Styles. I wear it for special occasions and important events, sort of like a good-luck charm. Fingers crossed it brings me good luck tonight.

When I kiss my Mom goodbye, she says, "I want you back here by ten o'clock."

Ugh. I'll bet any amount of money Walker doesn't have a curfew, and on the off chance he does, it's gotta be so much later than ten o'clock. "It's spring break, Mom. Can't I stay out until midnight?"

"If you're only doing algebra problems, then why do you need to stay out until midnight?"

She raises her eyebrows, daring me to contradict her. I'm already pushing my luck with this half-truth I told her, so instead of arguing, I walk out the door.

My annoyance at this early-curfew situation doesn't last long, though, because there's too much to be excited about. I practically bounce all the way to the subway station and spend the whole train ride fantasizing about how the night will go. Maybe we'll get some spumoni after our pizza, then take a long walk through the neighborhood. Maybe we'll play a game or two at the pool hall around the corner. Maybe he'll take me home at the end of the night. Maybe he'll kiss me.

I arrive at Spumoni Gardens five minutes early and scan the courtyard to see if he's already there. The outdoor dining area is a huge concrete slab crammed with picnic tables, enclosed by a chain-link fence. It's the farthest thing from fancy, but the pizza is out of this world.

It's unseasonably warm tonight, so most of the picnic tables are already full, and a line is forming at the pickup window. No sign of Walker, though. I lean against the fence and try not to seem too desperate as I look up and down Eighty-Sixth Street.

After a few seconds of silent waiting, I pull out my phone just to give myself something to do.

My thumb automatically taps the ZigZag icon, and I start scrolling through my feed. Memes, pictures, videos, repeat. It's the same stupid stuff all the time. Why was I so excited about this internship, anyway? I should delete the app already and be done with it.

A familiar scent distracts me from my mindless scrolling. That orangey-clovey cologne. I look up to see Walker smiling as he approaches. My stomach does a little backflip. "Hey," he says.

"Hey." I pocket my phone and smile back at him. "How's it going?"

"Good. You ready to eat?"

"Sure."

We wait on line for our Sicilian slices and cans of Pepsi, then find an unoccupied bench in the corner of the courtyard. The pizza is perfect, with a crust that's both crispy and tender, and there's a hint of spice in the rich tomato sauce. As we tuck into our meal, people chat and laugh all around us. In fact, it seems like the only two people who *aren't* talking in this whole courtyard are me and Walker.

The space between us is uncomfortably quiet. After yesterday's easy-flowing conversation, I'd expected us to pick up right where we left off. Instead, we're chewing in silence, avoiding eye contact, awkwardly sipping our sodas. It's got me thinking that yesterday was some sort of fluke. I test the waters with a simple icebreaker: "Where do you live?"

He looks like I've caught him by surprise. "Uh . . . this week, I'm living with my dad, on U and Third."

"Oh." I take a bite of pizza, waiting for him to tell me where he lives the other fifty-one weeks of the year. When he doesn't offer it up, I ask.

"My mom lives over near Brooklyn College with her boyfriend. I switch off every week. My parents are divorced. You know how it goes."

"Right." Except I don't really know how it goes, since my parents aren't divorced. They were never even married, and aside from those first six months of my life, I've never lived with my father. Sometimes I wonder if I have it easy, not having to split my life between two homes. At any rate, I'm *definitely* glad I don't have to live with Stefanie.

"Do you like your mom's boyfriend?" I ask.

He shrugs. "He's all right. At least he doesn't give me shit about my grades."

We descend back into silence and I rack my brain trying to think of something else to ask him. I should probably avoid delicate subject matter like grades or parents. This is a date. We should be having fun!

But what else is there to talk about? He and I don't have all that much in common. No mutual friends or shared interests—at least, none that I know of.

I'm about to make an inane comment on the weather when he saves me by asking a question of his own. "So, you're a tutor?"

It's a question he already knows the answer to, but it gives me an opening. "Yeah. Ms. Spiegel—you know, the head of the peer tutoring team?—she came to a math team meeting at the beginning of the year and asked if any of us would be interested in joining. I guess they have a shortage of tutors for algebra and geometry, so . . ." I trail off because Walker's looking at me funny. "What?"

"You're on the math team, too?"

"Uh-huh." I'm suddenly having flashbacks to Friday afternoon, with Jason telling me I spend too much time prepping for college and not enough time having fun. From the pinched expression on Walker's face, I'm pretty sure he'd agree.

Thing is, I *like* being on the math team. I like being on the peer tutoring team, and going to Coding Club, too. Sure, they'll look good on my college transcript, but more than that, they *are* fun. And I hate having to defend myself for liking them.

"I don't understand," he says. "What're you doing hanging out with me?"

Is he serious? "You *asked* me to hang out with you."

"Yeah, but why do you want to? You're, like, a genius. And I'm a screwup."

"You're not a screwup." I instinctively reach out my hand to offer him comfort, but quickly pull it back when I realize I'm being too forward. "I'm not a genius, either."

"Yes, you are. Name one class you're not totally acing."

That's easy. "History."

He looks incredulous and, if I'm not mistaken, a little impressed. "Did you fail Henley's midterm?"

"No, I got a B."

His face falls, like my passing grade is a disappointment. My failure to fail is somehow a failure in itself.

This conversation is proving to be more uncomfortable than the silence. Then, as if the situation could not get more awkward, I bite into my slice of pizza and a giant blob of thick red tomato sauce plops onto the front of my cream-colored sweater.

Damn.

I grab a flimsy paper napkin from the caddy on the table

and dab at the stain. It's a pointless exercise, as the napkin immediately disintegrates and the sauce seeps farther into the fabric. This sweater is probably ruined forever.

Walker doesn't seem to notice, though. He's staring into his can of Pepsi, his hazel eyes looking dull. He's turning inward again, like he did at the diner when his dad was chewing him out.

"I'm definitely a screwup," he says.

"No, you're not." I toss the balled-up napkin onto the table, like an exclamation point at the end of my sentence. "Look, we all have strengths and weaknesses. My strength just happens to be math. Math's not your strength, but so what? I'm sure you have something else you're really good at, or something you really love to do. What is it?"

The light returns to his eyes. "Art."

Finally, we're getting somewhere! "That's awesome. I haven't taken any art classes since our freshman-year requirement. Are you in the studio art program? I heard the audition process is brutal."

"Nah." He grimaces, as though the idea of taking an art class is repulsive. "I don't need that. I got my own thing going on."

"What kind of thing?"

He pops the last of his pizza into his mouth and swipes the crumbs from the palms of his hands. Then he swallows and says, "Tattoos."

"You're a tattoo artist?"

"Not officially. I'm not licensed or anything. But I've been hanging out in a shop and learning the ropes. I've started designing them, too."

"Do you have any yourself?"

He nods. "One on my back and one on my leg. They're

kinda hidden away. If my dad found out I had them, he'd be pissed. He doesn't like me hanging around the shop."

I can't imagine how horrified my mother would be if I came home with a tattoo. She'd probably never let me out of the house again. Still, I say, "I've always wanted to get a tattoo."

"Yeah?" He leans across the table, his perfect lips curled into a mischievous smile. "What kind of tattoo do you want?"

"I'm not sure." My mouth is dry and my heart's beating fast. Being close to Walker like this is giving me an adrenaline rush. "I haven't really given it much thought, I guess."

Walker's eyes burn into mine. "Why don't we swing by my shop? Maybe you'll find something you like."

I'm obviously not getting a tattoo tonight. First of all, I'm pretty sure you have to be eighteen to get a tattoo, which makes me wonder how Walker got his. Second, getting a permanent mark on my skin is not the kind of decision I want to make on the spur of the moment. Third, as I've already mentioned, my mother would ground me for life.

But I'm also not gonna tell Walker no.

It turns out the tattoo shop he frequents is right around the corner from Spumoni Gardens, in a tiny storefront nestled between the pool hall and a dry cleaner. A neon sign flashes in the window: GET INKED.

Inside, it's bright and tidy, much cleaner than I expected it to be. The air smells like a combination of disinfectant and incense, and the walls are lined with framed prints of tattoo designs, every kind you can possibly imagine: skulls, roses, spiderwebs, butterflies, hearts, daggers, birds, snakes. Some are pretty commonplace, like infinity signs. Others are, well . . . *unique,* like a topless woman riding a Pegasus.

"Yo!" Walker approaches the counter, where he slaps hands

with a big bearded guy wearing a bandanna tied around his head. I hang back while they talk and survey the designs on the walls, searching for something that sings to me.

I'm not getting a tattoo tonight. But if I were, what would it be? It would have to be meaningful, personal. A symbol that represents who I am and what's important to me.

"See anything you like?" Walker's next to me. His arm presses against mine and I press back.

"Not really."

"Mike's got a ton of books in the back. We can look through them until you find something."

"Okay. But . . ." I hesitate, afraid of sounding uncool. "I can't actually get a tattoo here, right? I mean, don't you have to be eighteen or whatever?"

He smirks and leans so close I can feel his breath on my ear. "Mike won't care. You're with me."

Then he wraps his strong arm around my shoulders and says, "It's my treat," and I am suddenly convinced that I need to get a tattoo tonight. I need to live in the moment and prove to Walker—to myself, to the entire universe—that I know how to have fun. I need it more than anything I've ever needed in my life.

We sit in the back room for a while, flipping through binder after binder of laminated flash. None of the designs are even remotely inspiring.

"You don't like this?" Walker says, pointing to a tiny pink heart with feathery wings. It could not be less representative of who I am or what's important to me.

"It's a contender," I say diplomatically, before sliding another thick book of designs off the shelf. This one's devoted solely to different styles of letters and numbers. Maybe I could get a word or a quote or something. I don't know what I'd get, though. Two days ago, I'd have gone for *Only you can control your future,* but now I know better.

I turn the pages, hoping for a sudden fit of inspiration, which I find about halfway through the binder. There's a page of lettering in a very familiar monospace font, the kind that's used in every code editor I've ever used. It kind of looks like the output of an old typewriter. A snippet of code would make for a meaningful, personal, unique tattoo. But I guess it wouldn't be very cool. I should probably get something fun.

Then it hits me. "I know what I want."

On a blank sheet of paper, I write out the following series of zeros and ones:

01000110
01010101
01001110

Each group of eight numbers represents a letter in binary code. In this case, there are three letters. *F. U. N.*

It's perfect.

My life doesn't have to be all work and no romance. I can be a good student and go out on dates. I can love to code and I can still have fun. It's not a binary choice.

"What's that?" Walker asks.

For some reason, I don't want him to know. "It's a secret code."

His eyes flash with admiration. Suddenly, I've gone from geeky to mysterious. "Where are you gonna get it?"

This is the tricky part. I can't get it anywhere my mom will see, but I'm not going to get half-naked in front of Walker and

Mike, either. My hair is long; when I wear it down, it falls well below my shoulders. I could easily hide a tattoo on the back of my neck. As long as I never wear another ponytail as long as I live.

Mike sits me down in a big reclining chair, kind of like the contraption I sit in when I go to the dentist. I roll over onto my side, with Walker perched on a stool right next to me. The tattoo machine buzzes to life, a grating drone that pierces my eardrums and makes my hair stand on end.

When the needle pricks my skin, I am instantly filled with regret. This is a mistake, a permanent one. I shouldn't have been so impulsive. My mother is going to kill me!

I grip my paper airplane pendant in one fist and squeeze my eyes shut, trying to block out the sharp, ceaseless pain. Then Walker takes my other hand, lacing his fingers through mine. I open my eyes and see him looking at me like I'm the coolest girl on the planet.

"Ashley," he says, "you are such a badass."

Like magic, the pain disappears. The buzzing of the motor fades away to nothing. Mike evaporates and the smell of disinfectant and incense is replaced with the scent of oranges and cloves.

I'm being impulsive, and probably making a huge mistake. But none of that matters now.

Because Walker Beech thinks I'm a badass.

And right about now, I feel like one, too.

Chapter Nine

I do not feel like a badass for very long.

By the time Mike finishes inking my neck, it's almost nine-thirty. I need to head home now or else I'm gonna blow curfew.

Walker's not leaving the shop anytime soon, though, because he's decided to get his very own spur-of-the-moment tattoo: a scorpion on his rib cage. "You inspired me," he says as he starts to take off his shirt.

I can't tear my eyes away from his fingers unclasping each tiny silver button. There is nowhere in the world I would rather be right now than in this room with a shirtless Walker Beech. But I remember the look on my mother's face when she told me to be home by ten o'clock. If I value the minimal freedom I have, I'd better do what she says.

"I've gotta go."

His fingers freeze halfway down the front of his shirt. "What? Why?"

There is no way I can admit how embarrassingly early my

curfew is. I'd go right back to being geeky instead of mysterious. Instead, I fumble over my words. "I can't stay. I've . . . got a thing . . . to do. Sorry, I just remembered."

He furrows his brow. I'm not sure if he's angry or disappointed or just plain confused, but I don't have the time to figure it out right now, so I say, "Text me later?" then run for the door before I can humiliate myself any further.

Thankfully, the N train arrives quickly. On the ride home, I replay the events of the evening in my head. It's really kind of amazing how quickly things escalated, isn't it? One minute I was dropping pizza sauce on my sweater, the next I was getting a tattoo.

I actually have a tattoo.

It almost doesn't feel real. The only reason I *know* it's real is because of the pain. It feels like a bad sunburn or a deep scrape. Fun searing right through my skin.

I walk through the door with two minutes to spare. Mom's sitting on the living room couch watching TV. "Where'd you go?"

"I told you, Spumoni Gardens."

She picks up her phone and taps the screen. "But then it says you went somewhere on Avenue U. You were there for over two hours."

Oh no. My phone location. How could I have forgotten? The back of my neck is throbbing as I throw out a plausible lie. "We were at the pool hall."

She raises her eyebrows. "What happened to algebra?"

"We finished early."

Mom sighs, clearly not buying it. She knows I was at the tattoo shop. She knows I got a tattoo.

This is it. My life is over.

"Look, Ashley," she says, "it's fine if you want to go on dates. You don't have to lie about that. But if you do go out with this boy again, I want to meet him. No excuses."

I hold my breath, waiting for the interrogation to continue.

"What's his name again?"

"Walker."

"How do you know him?"

"He's in my history class." I shrug one shoulder. "He's a nice guy."

"I'll be the judge of that. Next time, you bring him here. I mean it."

She turns her attention back to the television, so I guess she's done. Before she thinks of any other questions to ask, I retreat to my room and shut the door.

I got away with it! For a minute, I was half expecting her to sniff out the fresh tattoo ink.

My neck is still throbbing. I'm so curious to know what it looks like. After Mike finished, he let me steal a glance in the mirror, but then he wrapped it in a bandage and told me not to touch it for two hours. It's barely been one hour now, but I can't help myself. I want to see it.

I sweep my hair up into a topknot, then gently lift the dressing off the back of my neck. The cool air stings the open wound. Holding my phone behind me, I snap a photo, and my screen lights up with an image of my brand-new tattoo.

Zeros and ones, the language of computers, forever imprinted on my skin.

How badass is that?

...

It's been a while since I've slept in on a Monday, but the next morning, I do just that. In fact, I sleep until noon. There's nothing on my schedule for the day. No plans, no obligations. I could probably lie in bed until dinnertime.

Except I've gotta clean this tattoo. Mike said to do it twice a day, using gentle soap and water, followed by a fragrance-free moisturizer. As I swab it down, the skin feels raw to the touch. I take another photo, just to see how it's healing. It's red and slightly swollen. Supposedly, that's normal. Thankfully, Mom's at work, so I can wear my hair up for the rest of the day and give my neck some room to breathe.

I'm starting to feel bad for lying to her. Especially after seeing the sweet text she sent me a few hours ago: *There's ziti in the fridge, if you want it for lunch.* ♥

Walker sent me a text, too—at two in the morning. It's a close-up of his brand-new scorpion tattoo. I text back *Cool!*, but that's another lie, because I don't really think it's cool at all. It seemed fine when it was merely a drawing on a piece of paper. But set against his skin, it looks uncomfortably aggressive. There's even a drop of blood dangling from the tip of its stinger.

Meanwhile, my wearable project is still languishing in the corner, untouched and half-broken. I had big plans to fix it last night, but as soon as Walker asked me out, I forgot all about it. Now I cross the room and pick up the pieces—hoodie, circuit board, connective thread—determined to get these LEDs flashing by the end of the day.

After a half hour or so of tinkering, I think I pinpoint the source of the problem. I pull out a bunch of stitches and sew them back in a different order, only to find out I'm wrong. This happens a couple of times. Two hours later, I'm right back where I started—with a nonfunctioning hoodie.

Mr. P always says coding involves a lot of trial and error. You try a solution; if it doesn't work, you try something else. Over and over and over again. But as I sit here surrounded by wire fragments and about a thousand erroneous circuit diagrams, I can't help but feel I'm somehow deficient. Like I'll never succeed in being a software engineer, and ZigZag was right for rejecting me.

I'm redesigning my circuit for what seems like the fiftieth time when my phone dings with a text from Jason: *wanna help me with a prank?*

Weird. Jason hasn't asked for my help with a prank in a really long time. Not since before he started dating Rachel.

I'm in the middle of something.

cmon it won't take long
please? ☺

Another thing Mr. P always says is that it's good to take the occasional break, especially when you're frustrated. Sometimes, if you step away from your project and come back later with a fresh set of eyes, you'll be amazed at how quickly you can solve a problem that you previously thought was impossible.

I text back: *k.*

Ten minutes later, Jason knocks at my front door. He's holding a cheap blow-up doll with painted yellow hair and boobs shaped like traffic cones. "Do you have a dress I can borrow?"

"You're not putting my clothing on a blow-up doll."

"I'm not doing anything gross with her, I promise. I wanna dress her up and bring her out in public, then start talking to her like she's alive. I'm thinking about staging a fake argument, make it like she's breaking up with me or something. Do you think that's going too far?"

I'm struck with a vision of Jason walking down Ocean Parkway, arm in arm with this blow-up doll, and I burst into laughter. "Come in. I'll see if I can find something in her size."

He follows me down the hall and into my room, then lays the doll faceup on my bed. While I'm digging through my closet for the perfect ensemble, Jason says, "Whoa, what's this?"

I turn around to see him eyeing the circuitry on the floor. "It's my latest Coding Club project."

He leans down to inspect it. "What are you making?"

"A light-up hoodie. It's supposed to blink in time to music, but I'm having trouble getting it to work."

"That's so cool."

"Really? I figured you'd think it's one of those school-related things I do that's such a waste of my time."

He frowns. "This isn't a waste of time. I *wish* I could do something like this."

"You could. You just have to learn to code."

"Can you teach me how?"

"Well, this project is kind of advanced." His face falls, and I'm surprised by how much I hate seeing him disappointed. "I can show you something basic, though. Like 'Hello World.'"

"Hello World" is the classic programming example, a simple introduction to get your feet wet in whatever language you're learning: write a few lines of code to display those two words. Jason and I sit beside each other on the floor in front of my laptop, then I fire up my code editor and show him how to write his very first program.

I teach him the difference between a constant and a variable, and how to group his statements using curly braces, and why it's so important to leave concise, constructive comments. After a few minutes of typing, he finally gets the words *HELLO WORLD* to display on the screen in bold black letters.

"This is awesome!" He lets out a great big whoop and punches his fist in the air. I can't help but smile, because I remember how I felt after writing my first "Hello World" program. Like I was a total badass.

"How long did it take you to get good at this?" he asks.

"I started coding about two years ago," I say, though the way my hoodie is going, I'm not convinced I'm actually good at this.

His lip twitches as he looks at the screen. "I've got a lot of catching up to do."

"Don't worry, you'll catch up fast. There's a steep learning curve in the very beginning, but then it becomes like second nature. It's all about practice. You should join Coding Club. We're always looking for new members."

"Maybe I will." He shifts his gaze toward me, fixing me with his chocolate-brown eyes. "It'd be nice to hang out. I feel like I never see you anymore."

"We work together every weekend. And we see each other in Ms. Henley's class, like, every day."

"Yeah, but I mean fun stuff. We used to have so much fun."

"We did." And we both know why we don't anymore. Because as soon as he started dating Rachel, he stopped hanging out with me.

But do I want to bring that up? It'll make me look petty and jealous. Like I'm incapable of being happy for him. I look down at my lap, trying to think of the right words to say.

"What the hell is that?" Jason asks.

I glance around the room, but there's nothing amiss. "What are you talking about?"

"That!" He points to the back of my neck. "Did you get a tattoo?"

"Yeah. Do you like it?"

"What's it supposed to be?"

"It's binary. You know, the native language of a computer."

His eyes are wide and disbelieving. "When did you get that?"

"Last night, at this tattoo shop in Bensonhurst."

"Since when do you hang out in tattoo shops in Bensonhurst?"

I'm a little annoyed by his tone of voice. For someone who's planning to parade around in public yelling at a blow-up doll, he's being awfully judgmental. "I went with Walker."

He scowls. "What, is he your boyfriend now?"

Walker Beech is not my boyfriend. We've only been on one date, and we didn't even kiss. But I don't want to give Jason the satisfaction of knowing the truth. Because it seems like he's incapable of being happy for *me*. "What if he is?"

In an instant, he's on his feet. "Do what you wanna do. But I'm telling you, Ashley, Beech is trouble."

He snatches the blow-up doll before huffing out the door, slamming it behind him.

After he's gone, I realize he never took that dress he came for.

Chapter Ten

I sleep in on Tuesday, too. By the time I roll out of bed, it's 11:45, and there's a text waiting for me from Mom: *Clean your room today, it's a mess.*

She's not wrong. The still-broken hoodie and its various components are in a messy pile on my desk. Clothes and shoes and random junk are strewn across the floor. There are even some leftover scraps of my torn-up vision board floating around. Usually, I keep my bedroom super organized, but these last few days I've been letting it go.

According to the weather widget on my phone, it's sixty-eight degrees and sunny outside. It's the first real warm day of spring—unseasonably warm, even. I'm not gonna waste it cleaning my room.

I text Heaven and Christine.

> What are you guys up to today?

Heaven:
Making a packing list for PR.

I leave Saturday. 😔

Christine:
I've got nothing planned.
Just watching TV, scrolling thru ZigZag . . . the usual.
Wanna hang out?

Yes!
Let's go on a picnic!

Christine:
Ooooh yes!

Heaven:
👍 Where should we go?

The old Ashley would suggest someplace close by, like
Friends Field or Gravesend Park. The new Ashley needs to get
out of the neighborhood.

What about Prospect Park?

It takes about a half hour to get there on the F train. Only
a couple of miles away from home, but when I emerge from
the Fifteenth Street subway station, I might as well be in a different world.

I've been to this neighborhood before, on school trips to
the Brooklyn Museum and the Central Library. But I've never
actually gone inside Prospect Park, so I have no idea where
we should set up this picnic. Heaven knows her way around,
though. Apparently, her family has a membership to the

Brooklyn Botanic Gardens, and they come here all the time. Who knew?

She leads us down a long path, past playgrounds and barbecue areas, all of them crowded with kids since the whole New York City public school system is on spring break. Finally, we reach a huge stretch of grass that Heaven calls Long Meadow. We spread out a blanket and I plop down, staring up at the clear blue sky. It's hard to believe this much open space exists in the middle of Brooklyn.

Christine whips out her phone. "What're we listening to?"

"Taylor." Heaven and I say it at the same time.

A few seconds later, "The Man" is blasting from her tiny speaker. She sets the phone aside and starts unpacking her backpack. We follow suit, and soon there's a big pile of random snacks in the center of the blanket: granola bars, Doritos, Oreos, string cheese, popcorn. Lunch is served.

As I'm tearing into a package of cookies, Christine asks, "Did you get that email from the hackathon organizers?"

"The one where they announced the prizes?"

"Yeah." She turns to Heaven and explains. "First-place winners get these souped-up laptops. I really want one."

"Me too," I say. My laptop is approximately one thousand years old. It takes five minutes to boot up and freezes at random. My code editors won't run on it and it can't handle most modern web apps. If it weren't for the laptop I borrowed from Mr. P's workshop, I wouldn't be able to participate in the hackathon at all.

"Do you think we should see if anyone else wants to join our team?" Christine says. "More people means more brainpower."

"That's true, but I'm pretty sure everyone in Coding Club

has formed their teams already. We can always see if there's anyone willing to partner up once we get there, like Mr. P suggested."

She pulls a face. "I don't like the idea of working with a stranger. You know what it's like when you're stuck in a group project with people who don't pull their own weight. Who knows if we'll end up with some slacker?"

Heaven peels open a string cheese and nods. "Slackers are the worst."

"Maybe someone on math team would be interested," Christine says. "Or do you know someone on the peer tutoring team who'd be down? They don't have to know how to code, they just have to be willing to work hard."

"Let me think." I separate an Oreo and scrape the filling out with my teeth. Christine is right: even if you don't know how to code, there's always something you can contribute to the team, like brainstorming or testing or giving the presentation at the end. Still, it'd be nice to work with someone who has a basic understanding of coding. Someone who knows "Hello World."

"What about Jason?" I say.

"Jason Eisler?"

"Yeah. I know he seems like a weird choice, but I taught him some simple programming stuff yesterday and he picked up on it pretty fast."

Christine looks skeptical. "Jason's a notorious prankster. Would he take the hackathon seriously? I mean, this is a guy who set off a stink bomb in the cafeteria freshman year."

He's actually set off *two* stink bombs—one at the beginning of freshman year and one at the end of sophomore year—but

I'm not about to remind her of that. "I think he would take it seriously. He even said he was thinking about joining Coding Club."

She shrugs. "Okay. If you think he's really into it, ask him to join."

"Wait, back up," Heaven says. "Why were you hanging out with Jason yesterday? I thought you were into Walker Beech."

"It's not like that with Jason. We've known each other since we were babies. We're just friends."

"So what's going on with you and Walker, then? Any progress on the date situation?"

A smile spreads across my face. "We went out on Sunday night."

Heaven squeals. "Tell me everything! How did it go? What did you do? Is he a good kisser?"

"Well . . ." My smile droops a little. "We didn't actually kiss. I had to leave early. It was kind of weird how it happened."

I launch into the tale of my first date with Walker. As the story goes on, the girls' eyes get progressively wider. When I sweep my hair aside to show them the back of my neck, they let out a collective gasp.

"Shut up!" Christine says.

"You did *not* get a tattoo." Heaven reaches out to touch it and I recoil.

"Don't," I say. "It's still healing."

"That is *so* cool," Christine says. "I want a tattoo in binary now. My parents would kill me, though."

"My mom has no idea, and I need to keep it that way."

"Did Walker get a tattoo?" Heaven asks.

"Yeah." I'm not sure I want to tell them about the scorpion with the bloody stinger. It's sort of embarrassing. Then again, it might be good to see what they think. It's entirely possible I'm reading this situation wrong. I pull out my phone to show them the photo Walker sent me. "This is it."

Heaven smiles politely and doesn't say a thing. Christine says, "Uh . . . that's kind of aggressive."

I dim my phone screen. "I was thinking the same thing."

"Does he come off as, like, a hostile dudebro or anything?" Heaven asks.

"No, he's actually really sweet. And I know he was afraid of his dad finding out."

Christine rolls her eyes. "It's an immature act of rebellion. He probably thinks this makes him look tough."

"I wonder if Shawn has any tattoos." Heaven gets a dreamy look in her eyes and stares off into the distance.

"Do you ever interact with him outside of Roll-N-Roaster?" Christine asks.

"Yeah, on ZigZag."

"You guys are ZigZag friends?"

"No." She chews thoughtfully on her cheese stick. "It's more of a one-sided interaction, if you know what I mean."

"So you stalk him."

"Pretty much."

"You know, he's graduating soon," I say. "If you wanna make your move, you're running out of time."

She sighs dramatically. "What am I supposed to do? Send him a message out of nowhere? He'll think I'm a stalker."

"One: you *are* a stalker," I say. "Two: it wouldn't be coming out of nowhere. You talked to him on Saturday night. Just continue the conversation."

"Okay." She takes her phone from the front pocket of her backpack. "Help me figure out what to write."

"You were talking to him about having fun over spring break, right? Making sure he set his priorities."

Heaven nods and confidently taps out a message: *did you get your priorities in order yet?* 😌

I give her a thumbs-up, and she hits Send.

As she scrolls through her ZigZag feed, it strikes me that I've never seen Walker's profile. He and I aren't ZigZag friends, which is weird. I mean, we've gone on a date. Technically, that's "dating," isn't it?

But when I search for the name "Walker Beech," it comes up empty. "He probably has a secret profile," Christine says. "Like a finsta, where he keeps his friends list really small."

If that's true, I guess I didn't make the cut.

Suddenly, Heaven squeals. "Omigod, he wrote back! He said, 'What do you mean?' Obviously, he doesn't remember anything I told him the other night."

"So remind him."

She takes a deep breath and speaks as she types. "I mean, are you having fun yet?" A moment later, she squeals again. "He says he went to a party last night."

This time, she types silently, and from the smile radiating across her face, it quickly becomes clear that she and Shawn are engaged in a riveting conversation. Christine leans back, closing her eyes against the warm spring sun, as the music on her phone transitions to "Wildest Dreams."

I wonder what Walker's doing right now.

We haven't talked since that last text exchange about his tattoo. Though it wasn't really much of an exchange. He texted at two in the morning, I wrote back at noon the next day, and that was it. Maybe I should take my own advice and be more proactive.

I text him: *What're you up to today?* Then I stare at my screen, waiting for a response that never comes.

"Omigod, Shawn sent pictures of this party," Heaven says. "You've gotta check them out, they're insane."

The three of us huddle together over her phone as she scrolls through the photos. It looks like a stereotypical house party, the kind I never get invited to. A dozen people piled together on a couch, red Solo cups in hand. Beer pong on a kitchen table. Vaping on a back stoop.

"I don't recognize any of these people," Christine says.

"He said it was hosted by his friend who goes to Edmund's."

St. Edmund's is the Catholic school on Ocean Avenue. I don't know anyone who goes there, so I'm rapidly losing interest in these photos.

"Um . . . isn't that Walker?" Heaven taps an action shot of a guy slamming a beer bong. It's definitely not Walker.

"No. That guy's got red hair."

"Not him. The guy in the background." She zooms in, and sure enough, there's Walker. His mouth is open, like he's laughing at a really funny joke. He's holding a bottle of beer in one hand.

And his other arm is wrapped around the shoulders of a beautiful girl.

"Who is that?" Heaven says. "And why does he have his arm around her?"

I swallow hard, unable to speak. We may not know who that girl is, but we all know why he's got his arm around her. Because he's Walker Beech, the most gorgeous guy in the borough of Brooklyn, and he's totally out of my league. He doesn't really like me. I was an idiot to think he did. I'm not cool or mysterious, I'm just some desperate loser who chased him down the street and got a geeky tattoo to try to impress him.

Clearly, he wasn't impressed.

Heaven puts her hand on my arm. "You okay?"

My vocal cords are frozen. It's just the three of us here on this picnic blanket, but somehow, I feel like everyone who attended this party last night is watching me. Judging me. Laughing at how stupid I was to think I actually had a chance with Walker Beech, when girls who look like *that* walk the streets of Brooklyn.

"Don't let him upset you," Christine says. "He's an immature jerk. He's not even worth it."

"Seriously." Heaven dims her phone screen, erasing that horrible picture from view. "Screw him."

They're right. He's a jerk. Screw him.

Still, I'm completely humiliated. I made such a big deal about how I was going to take control of my love life, but obviously, I can't control it any more than I can control whether I get into my first-choice college.

And you know what? Even if good grades don't guarantee a successful future, at least they make me feel good about myself. Like I've accomplished something if I get an A. Now, I feel nothing but shame and hurt and embarrassment. And I've got nothing to show for it except an impulsive tattoo.

Dating is highly overrated. And it *definitely* isn't fun.

Chapter Eleven

om was annoyed that I went to Prospect Park yesterday instead of cleaning my room, so now I'm banned from leaving the apartment until I get it done. Which honestly is fine with me. It's not like I want to go anywhere or do anything or see anyone. I'd much rather be home alone, where I can mope around and feel sorry for myself in peace.

That doesn't mean I'm actually cleaning, though. I can't bring myself to get up off my bed. I'm just lying here, staring at the ceiling, regretting every choice I've ever made.

My phone dings three times, in quick succession. A string of texts pop up on my screen, and when I see they're from Walker, my stomach clenches.

> hey
> wut r u up to now?
> wanna come over?

He has got to be kidding. I haven't heard from him since our date, and now he expects me to drop by his house on a moment's notice? No way. I've got more important things to do. Like lie here and stare at the ceiling.

I type *You're a jerk,* then delete it. I type *Screw you,* then delete that, too. What I really want to type is *Who was that girl you were with at that party on Monday night?* Instead, I type *I'm in the middle of something,* and hit Send.

He responds, *plz?* and I remain unmoved, until he follows up with, *i rly need to c u.* Those six abbreviated words rip right through my fragile armor. Sure, Walker Beech is a jerk, but he *needs to see me.* How can I ignore that?

Leaving the apartment isn't an option, though, since Mom is using her phone to stalk my every move. She won't be home for at least three, maybe four, hours, so I text him, *Come to my place instead.* He replies with a thumbs-up. Finally, the motivation I need to clean my room.

I spend the next fifteen minutes tidying up, then the fifteen minutes after that making myself look presentable. I slip on this cute graphic tee that says MADE IN BROOKLYN and style my hair into a fishtail braid using a video tutorial I found on Zig-Zag. After I slick on a coat of pale pink lip gloss, I take stock of my reflection in the mirror.

That girl in the picture is so much prettier than me.

I'm about to text Walker to call the whole thing off when the buzzer blares. He's already here, in the lobby. I press the button to let him in, then hold my breath until I hear the knock at my front door.

"Hey." His hazel eyes are apologetic. Like he's not sure he should be here.

"Hey." I'm not sure he should be here, either.

But I invite him in anyway.

I don't bring him back to my bedroom. We sit at the kitchen

table, me in my mom's usual spot and him in mine. His hands are clasped and he's staring down at them. He's so gorgeous. What is he *doing* here?

"So . . . ," I say. "Why did you need to see me?"

He clears his throat, then clears it again. "It's my dad. He's giving me shit again. About the extra credit for Franzen."

Oh. I know where this is going.

He doesn't need to *see* me. He needs me to *do* something for him. There's a huge difference between those two needs.

"I haven't done anything yet," he says. "I really need some help."

It's impossible to find the words to respond. I feel like my chest might explode. Maybe it will, and then I won't have to say anything at all. We'll just sit here covered in the bloody remnants of my obliterated heart.

"You said you'd help me," he says. "Remember?"

Suddenly, the words reveal themselves. "I'm only good enough for you to text when you need something from me?"

He looks wounded. "But . . . you offered."

"I haven't heard from you since Sunday. Where've you been?"

"Nowhere. Around."

"I texted you yesterday and you never responded."

"I'm sorry. I guess I forgot."

"Who was that girl at the party?"

"What party?"

"On Monday night. You had your arm around a girl. Is she your girlfriend or something?"

"Wait." His eyes narrow. "You were there?"

"No, my friend was." My voice sounds squeaky and off-balance, because I realize this makes me sound like I've deployed an army of spies to report back to me on his where-abouts. Quickly, I add, "It was a total coincidence. Anyway, she showed me some pictures and you were in one of them. With your arm around that girl."

He pulls at the edge of his earlobe. "That was Candice. My ex. She goes to Edmund's. I wasn't planning to hang out with her that night, she was just there. She got drunk and started hanging all over me and I didn't want to tell her to back off because then she'd get upset and it would've been a whole drama."

His explanation seems reasonable. People can be messy drunks, or so I've been told. It's not like I ever hang out in situations where people get drunk. I've never been drunk myself, either.

Though, in the photo, she wasn't so much hanging on *him* as he was hanging on *her*. Still, it was one moment in time, a fragment of a second captured in a frame. It doesn't tell the whole story.

It's hard to know whether to believe him. I don't know him well enough to trust him. But I *want* to trust him. And maybe that's enough.

"Why do you care, anyway?" he asks.

The question catches me off guard. "What's that supposed to mean?"

"You ran off the other night as soon as you got your tattoo. Said you needed to be somewhere else." His eyes fall to his fingers fidgeting with the edge of the tablecloth. "I figured you had something better to do than hang out with me."

The puzzle pieces snap together in my head, and I can't help but laugh. "That is so the opposite of what actually happened." He frowns and I say, "I left because I had to go home.

My mom's really strict and I have an early curfew, but I was too embarrassed to admit that to you."

I thought this would make him laugh, too—What a silly misunderstanding!—but he's still frowning. Like the concept of a curfew is completely confusing.

"I'm sorry you thought I was blowing you off," I say, reaching my hand across the table. "I really wanted to stay. I promise."

His frown softens and he takes my hand. "The scorpion turned out awesome. Mike did such a good job on the linework. Especially around the stinger, right?"

"Right." An image of that dangling blood droplet flashes through my mind. "I'm curious, why did you pick that scorpion? Does it have some special meaning to you, or . . ." *Are you secretly a hostile dudebro?*

He shrugs. "I just think it looks cool."

This is the best answer I could've hoped for. "Cool."

"So," he says, his fingers tightening around mine, "is everything good with us, then?"

"Absolutely." I'm so ready to move on from this whole mess. "Should we get to work on your extra credit?"

He breathes out hard, like he's been holding it for our entire conversation. "Yeah. That'd be great."

"Where is it? Did you bring it with you?"

"No, it's all online. My laptop's not working. I was hoping we could use yours."

"Uh, sure. Lemme get it." I retreat to my room to grab the laptop I borrowed from Mr. P's workshop, because I don't feel like sitting around waiting for my ancient one to boot up. You'd think if Franzen was going to give an online assignment, he'd have made sure Walker had the tech to get it done. I guess not every teacher is as thoughtful as Mr. P.

We load the assignment on the laptop and I scroll through to see what we're dealing with. These questions aren't super-hard; we'll be able to get through them in the next couple of hours, as long as we focus. I set some scrap paper and a couple of pencils in front of Walker, just like I do with any other student I tutor.

"Let's go through these problems one by one," I say. "Show me how you would approach each solution, and I'll help you whenever you get stuck. Start with number one."

He squints at the screen, reading the first question. It's a fairly straightforward polynomial equation. After a couple of seconds, he shakes his head. "I don't know."

"Well, how do you think you'd start?"

Another shake of the head. "I have no idea."

"You have to find the greatest common factor."

He gives me this blank stare and I realize this is going to take more than a couple of hours.

"Let me show you." I slip a piece of scrap paper from the pile in front of him and give a basic overview of how to factor polynomials. The sheet is promptly filled with xs and ys and parentheses and equal signs. Out of the corner of my eye, I see Walker picking up his pencil too. Great! He's following along, taking notes.

When I finish my mini-lesson, I glance over at his paper to check on his progress. He's not taking notes at all. He's doodling. Instead of xs and ys, he's drawn a fire-breathing dragon. Admittedly, it's really good, but I also feel like I wasted the last five minutes of my life yammering on about algebra to someone who couldn't care less.

"Did you get any of that?" I ask.

His pencil stops moving and he catches my eye. I throw a

meaningful look down at his paper, and his hand covers the drawing, like he's embarrassed. "Sorry. I just got this really good idea for a design. When I'm bored, I start drawing."

I wonder if he doodles his way through all his classes. It makes me think that all those times I thought he was studiously taking notes in American History, he was really just designing tattoos. "Look, I get that you hate this subject, but if you want to bring your grade up, you're gonna have to do this. At least try, okay?"

"Okay." He sits up straight and leans closer to me. "How do I solve this first problem?"

If he'd been paying attention, he'd know exactly how to solve it. I'm about to tell him that, but all of a sudden, he wraps his arm around my shoulders, and his cologne wafts into my nostrils and attacks my common sense.

There are twenty questions on this extra credit assignment. What harm would it do if I answered one? Just to give him some forward momentum.

I type the answer into the text box on the screen—$(x+1)(x+4)$—and hit Next.

For question two, I try again to engage him in the subject. I write out examples and explain everything in the simplest terms I can. He's not doodling anymore—it's kind of hard for him to do that with his arm around me—but I still can't tell if he's paying attention. That dreamy, mysterious aura that makes me melt whenever he walks into a room also makes him a really difficult person to tutor.

This time, though, I refuse to give him the answer. I make him talk through his thoughts, slowly and steadily, as I take notes on scrap paper. It's frustrating and unpleasant, but eventually, he finds the right solution. When he types it in the text box with his own two hands—$9x^4y^2$—he's practically beaming. It's a major victory.

It also takes forty-five minutes.

The third question is harder. Walker's patience is dwindling. At one point, he pulls away from me and rakes his hands through his hair with a groan. It's painful. To spare us any further agony, I type the answer into the text box—$\log_4 10$—and hit Next.

We're just getting started on the fourth question when Mom texts: *On my way home!* Time for Walker to get out of here. I don't even want to think about how much trouble I'll be in if she finds out I've been home alone with him all day.

"We'd better wrap this up for today." I save our progress and snap my laptop shut, feeling both disappointed and relieved. It's been incredible spending so much time in such close proximity to Walker, but I kind of wish there was less algebra involved. "We can keep going tomorrow, if you want."

"Yeah, sure."

I stand up, but Walker stays seated. He's staring at my laptop with his mouth half-open. Did I forget to save our progress or something? "Is everything okay?"

He looks up at me with pleading eyes. "Can I take your laptop home?"

Without a second thought, I say, "No. It's not mine, it's Mr. P's. But we can totally use it again when you come over tomorrow."

"But I want to go over our work tonight so I'm more prepared for our next session." His eyes turn from pleading to desperate. "Please, Ashley?"

I don't know Walker well enough to trust him. I don't know for sure if he'll protect my laptop from harm. But he seems like he's trying, and I *want* to trust him. I hope that's enough.

"Okay," I say. "But you have to promise me you'll bring it back tomorrow. Don't use it for anything besides your extra credit. And guard it with your life."

"I promise." He grabs it from the table, casually tucking it under his arm like a football. It takes all my willpower not to reach out and snatch it back.

This is a huge mistake. I need to tell him I changed my mind.

He smiles that gorgeous smile, and suddenly I can't speak. "You're amazing, Ashley. Seriously. I can't thank you enough."

Then he leans forward and kisses my lips. It's a chaste kiss. Quick, closed mouth, no tongue. But it's the first lip-on-lip action I've ever had with a boy. Technically, this is my first kiss. Isn't it?

This is a momentous occasion. Or it should be. The truth is, it all feels a little anticlimactic. I'd been expecting something bigger for My First Kiss, something slightly more explosive. Not a half-hearted peck. And now Walker's running down the hallway like he can't get away from me fast enough.

When he disappears into the stairwell, I close the front door and stand there for a really long time, staring at the dead bolts as if they can tell me what just happened here. I'm dying to text Heaven and Christine to see what they think, but if I tell them I loaned him my laptop, they'll probably freak out on me.

The scent of Walker's cologne is still lingering in the air when someone knocks at the door. He's back! He must've realized that kiss was inadequate and he's returned to give me a proper one. I lick my lips and throw open the door, ready for my do-over. But it's not Walker. It's Jason.

"Oh." It's hard to hide the disappointment in my voice.

Jason can sense it. "Gee, it's good to see you, too."

"Sorry, you just surprised me. What's up?"

He holds up his phone. There's a big red button on the screen and a glimmer in his eyes. "Press the button," he says.

I indulge him and tap the screen. An obnoxious fart noise fills the room.

"This is why you came here? To show me an app that makes fart noises?"

"I made it."

"You made what?"

"This." He presses the button again and I wince at the sound. "The fart app."

"You mean, you coded it yourself?"

"Yeah." His smile is so wide now. "I know it's stupid, and it's been done about a billion times already, but I've been messing around with this app development software I found on the internet, and this was an easy first project to do. What do you think?"

"I think it's awesome." I'm not just saying that either; I'm genuinely impressed. He only started coding last week, and now look at him, making his own fart app. "How long did it take you to do this?"

"Most of today. You were right, it gets easier the more you do it. And I know this sounds weird, but it's kind of addictive."

"No, I know exactly what you mean. Once you realize what you can do with a few lines of code—"

"—you never wanna stop."

We both laugh. It feels nice to connect with him again. Jason and I used to finish each other's sentences all the time.

"You know," I say, "I was talking with Christine the other day, and we'd really like to add some more members to our hackathon team."

"What's a hackathon?"

"It's basically a marathon coding competition. It's happening next weekend and we were wondering if you'd like to join us."

"Me?" He furrows his brow. "But I barely know anything."

"Anyone of any skill level can compete. You're clearly a quick learner, and I think you'd help our chances of winning. The more brainpower, the better."

"What do you win?"

"First prize is a supernice laptop. Second prize is a smart-watch. I think third place is a drone or something."

His eyes light up. "Oh, I could pull so many good pranks with a drone. I'll do it."

"Awesome! I'll send you the link to sign up."

"Cool." He nods and we descend into this slightly awkward silence. I can tell something's wrong because his lip twitches the tiniest bit. Maybe he's feeling insecure about the hack-athon. I'm about to launch into a pep talk, but then he says, "You seen Beech lately?"

Why is he so obsessed with Walker Beech?

"Yeah," I say. "He was here today, actually."

"Does your mother know that?"

"No, and we're not gonna tell her."

"What do you see in him, anyway?"

That's easy: his flawlessly tousled hair, and his dazzling hazel eyes, and his impeccable hands. But I need to give Jason an answer that has nothing to do with Walker's physical appearance. Something less superficial.

"He's fun," I say, even though what we did today was the polar opposite of fun.

"Fun? So, like, hanging out in a tattoo shop is fun for you now?"

"At least it's something out of the ordinary. I feel like my entire life is confined to a one-mile radius. Sometimes I forget I even live in New York City."

Jason frowns. "I just don't think he sounds like he knows how to have fun."

"And you do?"

"Yeah, actually, I do." Jason draws back his chest, like he's readying for battle. "You want fun? I'll show you fun. We're going out tonight."

"We are?"

"Yeah."

"And where are we going?"

"It's a surprise."

"Are you bringing me out on a date with your blow-up doll? Because I'm not in the mood to be a third wheel."

The tips of his ears go bright pink. "No, I promise. It's not a prank. You'll like it."

"Okay." I kind of love the idea of Jason planning a surprise. He really does know how to have fun, even if I won't admit that to him now. "What should I wear?"

"Dress casual," he says, a smile spreading across his face. "Bring a jacket. And wear comfortable shoes."

Chapter Twelve

Jason knocks on my door at six forty-five. We'd planned to meet in the lobby at seven, so I'm not sure why he's here fifteen minutes early. I haven't even finished drying my hair yet.

While I wrap things up in my room, Mom happily sits with him at the kitchen table. She loves Jason, despite the fact that he's always getting in trouble.

When my hair's done and my lip gloss is applied, I grab my jacket and bag and step out into the hallway. Snippets of conversation echo from the kitchen. Mom says "so important," and Jason says "trying harder." She's probably nagging him about his grades or something. I hurry into the kitchen to save him.

Wow. Jason's dressed up. Not black-tie-fancy or anything, but I'm so used to seeing him in ratty tees and ripped jeans that the Henley he's wearing might as well be a tuxedo. He told me to dress casual, but this outfit is more like *smart* casual. I wish he'd been more specific.

And did he put product in his hair? Since when does he put product in his hair? It looks good.

"Should I go change?" I ask.

He takes in my jeans and sweater and Converse. "Why? You look great."

"Are you sure? I don't want to be underdressed for wherever it is we're going."

"Nah. You're dressed perfectly."

My mom raises her eyebrows. "You don't know where you're going?"

"Jason's surprising me." I try to make my voice as sarcastic as possible to hide the fact that I'm actually really excited.

She looks from me to him and back again, a smile slowly spreading across her face. "How sweet!"

"It's not like that, Mom." I think she's secretly hoping we'll fall in love with each other and start dating. I wonder if Jason's parents think the same thing. How embarrassing.

Jason looks as uncomfortable as I feel. Time to get this show on the road.

"Ready?" I say.

"Ready." He stands up and follows me to the front door.

"Have her home by ten o'clock," Mom calls after us, and Jason responds, "Aye-aye."

I slam the door closed behind us and huff out a breath. "Sorry about that."

"Nothing to apologize for," he says. "Your mom's cute."

"*Cute* is one word for it." As we wait for the elevator, a familiar scent floods the hallway. Like an orange studded with cloves. "Are you wearing new cologne?"

He clears his throat. "Yeah. Is it okay?"

"Totally. I love that scent." Except I love that scent on Walker, so now I'm confused. And kinda weirded out. Because I'm having this Pavlovian response right now, a feeling of . . . I dunno. Longing? Desire? But this is *Jason*. I don't think of him that way. It's not like that between us. It never has been.

The door rumbles open in the lobby and we're on the sidewalk before I realize I don't know which way we're headed. "Where to now?"

"This way," he says, and takes my hand.

Jason's taken my hand like this a million times before, whether leading me on a hunt for PokéStops in the cemetery or pulling me into a hiding spot so we can secretly spy on the victims of his pranks. This should be a nonevent. But the moment his skin touches mine, I get a squirmy feeling in my stomach. My ankles start to wobble a little, and I have to suppress an urge to giggle.

This cologne must be messing with me. Would it be rude to hold my nose?

As we start down the street, I wriggle my hand free from his grasp. This is too weird. Too much.

"Where are we going?" I ask.

"The F train."

"Are we taking it into the city?"

There's a subtle glimmer in his eye when he says, "You'll see."

I never go to Manhattan at night. I mean, I hardly go to Manhattan at all, but when I do, it's usually during the day, to visit a museum or see a show or do some shopping. Nightlife just isn't my thing. Some kids at school like to go to this one particular club in the Village because apparently the doorman is really lax about letting people in with fake IDs. Is that where he's planning to take me tonight?

"I don't have a fake ID, Jason."

"You don't need a fake ID." He looks insulted. "Where do

you think we're going? I would never take you to a club. I know you hate that kind of thing. Plus, your mom would kill me if she found out."

"Right." That's a relief. Sort of.

A few minutes ago, I was really excited about being surprised, but now the not knowing is making me nervous. I like to be prepared and informed at all times. Getting on an F train without a clear destination in mind makes me feel like I'm jumping off a diving board with a blindfold on, not sure whether I'll land in a warm saltwater pool or a mud pit.

Jason can tell I'm nervous, because he says, "Just relax. I promise I won't get you into any trouble."

At the subway station, we swipe our MetroCards and run up the stairs in time to catch an arriving Manhattan-bound F train. The car is half-empty, and there's a two-seater in the corner with our names on it.

"Will you at least tell me where we're getting off?"

"I'll tell you when we get there." When I narrow my eyes at him, he says, "If I tell you now, it'll ruin the surprise. Can't you just trust me?"

I open my mouth to argue but find there's no argument to be had. I've known Jason forever, and he's never given me a reason not to trust him. Even my mom trusts him, and she doesn't trust anybody.

"What was my mom harassing you about back there?" I ask.

"She wasn't harassing me. I was telling her how excited I am about this hackathon." He runs his hand over his product-enhanced hair. "I'm a little nervous, though."

"Why?"

"Well, you and Christine are so good, and I don't really know what I'm doing. Aren't you afraid I'll bring your team down?"

"If I was, do you really think I would have invited you to join us? Don't worry, we'll show you what to do. It won't be hard."

"It won't be hard for *you,* Ms. Future Software Engineer." He nudges my foot with the tip of his sneaker. A playful gesture, but I can't seem to muster a smile. Because who knows if I'll ever be a software engineer. ZigZag doesn't seem to think I'm up to the task.

"Did I say something wrong?"

"No." The word comes out unsteady and I shake my head, and suddenly there's a lump in my throat and oh god please don't cry right now, Ashley.

Jason leans forward and squeezes my hand, his eyes filled with concern. "What is it? What did I say?"

Before any tears can fall, I wipe my eyes with the back of my other hand, the one he's not squeezing. "Nothing," I say, sniffling back a sob. I cannot let myself cry on the subway. "It's not you. There was this program I applied for, an internship at ZigZag. It's at their headquarters in Silicon Valley, and—"

"I know. You told me all about it," he says. "I do listen when you talk, you know."

"Oh." Of course I've mentioned it to Jason. It's been all I've been talking about for weeks. I didn't realize he remembered, though. I should've given him more credit. "Well, I thought I was a shoo-in, but they rejected me."

"I'm so sorry." He rubs the back of my hand with his thumb, a soft, subtle, comforting touch.

"Now I feel like maybe I don't have what it takes to be a software engineer. Maybe I won't get into the colleges I want to go to, either. I used to be so sure about everything, but lately it feels like my future is totally out of my control."

I wipe my eyes again. The people across from us are looking at me now. How humiliating.

Jason's still rubbing the back of my hand, though, and it's helping me to breathe easier. I feel calmer, warmer. Less anxious.

"Your future *is* out of your control," he says. "You can't force things to go your way all the time. All you can do is try your best. But it's just one summer program. It doesn't define the rest of your life. You're the smartest person I know, Ashley, and you can be anything you want to be. One day, ZigZag's going to realize they made a huge mistake."

This is the sweetest thing he's ever said to me. "Thank you."

"I mean it. And I'm sorry for what I said last week, about you not making enough time to have fun. The truth is, I admire how hard you work and how seriously you take everything. It's what makes you *you*. So don't ever try to change yourself. Not for me, and not for . . . anyone else."

His gaze drops, just for a moment, and I know that by "anyone else," he means Walker. Then he looks into my eyes again and I have an overwhelming urge to bury my face in his chest, to breathe in his pomander scent. But then the train pulls into the Jay Street station, and he hops to his feet, still holding my hand. "Let's go."

We run across the platform to the A train, which is insanely crowded. Fortunately, we only take it one stop, to High Street. The last stop in Brooklyn.

There are a lot of stairs to climb at this station. It empties out onto a busy street, with a big park on one side. The spring night is darker and chillier than it was at the start of this journey, but my blood is pumping so fast and hard, I have to take off my jacket to avoid breaking out in a sweat.

He's dragging me through the park now, past what looks like a war memorial. To our right, orange construction cones surround an open trench, and in the distance, there's an official-looking building all lit up. It could be a courthouse, or maybe that's Borough Hall. It's kind of amazing how I've lived in Brooklyn my entire life, yet there's so much of it I haven't seen. So much I don't know about.

"Okay, *now* will you tell me what we're doing?"

He leads me to an island in the center of a busy street. There's a white sign above our heads, with icons of a wheelchair, a stick figure, a bicycle. It reads: TO MANHATTAN.

His eyes glimmer as he says, "We're gonna walk across the Brooklyn Bridge."

Chapter Thirteen

This is, without a doubt, the best surprise.

"Make sure you stick to the pedestrian side of the white line," he says. "You don't wanna get run over by a bike."

He eases me forward, his hand on the small of my back, as we make our way along the path. It's a concrete walkway with elevated guardrails to protect people from the traffic zooming by on either side. I've never walked across the Brooklyn Bridge. From where we're standing, I can't see it, but Jason assures me it's just ahead and to the left.

"Have you done this before?" I ask. He seems confident, like he knows exactly where he's going. Granted, there's a big green sign that says BROOKLYN BRIDGE with two arrows pointing in the direction we're headed. But still, there's this casual self-assurance in his step that makes me feel totally comfortable following him wherever he leads me.

"Once," he says. "A while ago. Rachel recorded me photobombing tourists."

"Oh, right. I saw that video."

Real talk? It wasn't his best work. The concept was funny—

who wouldn't laugh at a good photobomb?—but it didn't feel like "authentic Jason." The video was way overproduced. Lots of weird transitions and unnecessary special effects. There was this loud background music, too. All of it distracted me from the best part of the show: Jason.

"It wasn't one of my favorites," he says. "You know what's crazy, though? It's my best-performing video, by far. Got over ten thousand views and counting."

"Whoa."

"Yeah, I know." He shakes his head. "Rachel really knows what she's doing. I had wanted to put up a straight edit of the photobombs, but she insisted on adding all the graphics and music and stuff. She said it would get me more hits, and she was right. But it didn't feel . . . what's the word?"

"Authentic?"

"Exactly! Authentic. Plus, she said I needed to work on my 'onscreen presence.'" He rolls his eyes and bends his fingers into sarcastic air quotes.

"That's crazy! Your comedic timing is stellar, and you look great on camera. You're a natural."

"I look great on camera, huh?" He purses his lips in a perfect impression of Zoolander's Blue Steel, and I can't contain my laughter. Jason's laughs are stilted, though. "Rachel always said my pranks should be more ZigZag-friendly, to get more views and channel subscribers. You know how she is with her ZigZag profile: it's all about likes and follows. But I kind of hated it. She didn't really get me."

"I thought she was your number one fan."

He turns his head to look at me, his dark-brown eyes shining in the streetlights. "Nah. She wanted me to be someone I'm not."

"Well, you should never change yourself for anyone," I say. "Someone once told me that. I forget who, though."

Jason nudges me playfully with his elbow. I giggle, but I'm genuinely upset about this. How could Rachel not appreciate him for who he is? He's one of the funniest, most free-spirited, and entertaining people I know. Not to mention thoughtful, as evidenced by this wonderful evening he planned for us. And now that I think about it, he's pretty cute, too. I'll bet he was an excellent boyfriend.

It's funny: I've been friends with him for what feels like forever, and until now, I've never once thought about him like *that*. Must be the cologne.

"Rachel doesn't know what she's talking about," I say. "One day, she'll realize she made a huge mistake, and she'll be sorry she let you go."

He shrugs, like it doesn't bother him all that much. "We were doomed from the start. The two of us had nothing in common. No basis for a lasting relationship."

"Right."

What do Walker and I have in common? Not much, aside from the fact that we both have tattoos. I remember how hard it was to come up with something to talk about at Spumoni Gardens. Maybe this means we're already doomed.

"Come on, let's pick up the pace." Jason hooks his pinkie around mine, then leads me down the promenade. Holding his hand doesn't feel weird anymore. It feels warm and familiar. Comfortable.

Eventually, One World Trade comes into view, its antenna glowing silvery against the starless sky. Then, as we turn left, the first of the bridge's two suspension towers appears. There are brightly lit cables on either end and, at the very top, an

American flag ripples in the breeze. The closer we get, the more downtown buildings appear, none of which I can identify individually. Together, though, they unmistakably form the New York City skyline.

We walk without speaking, listening to the whoosh of the cars that are now below us. I'm surprised by how crowded the promenade is, though I know I shouldn't be. This is the city that never sleeps, and it's barely eight o'clock on a Wednesday night. Of course the Brooklyn Bridge is crowded.

As we approach the first tower, the crowd gets even bigger. Every few feet, someone stops to take a photo or to gape at the scenery. But we keep moving forward, our pinkies still locked together, until we're standing in the shadow of the two pointed arches.

Jason steers me beneath the left arch, toward a platform that protrudes over the Brooklyn-bound highway. It's a popular spot for photo ops, so a lot of people are gathered here, but there's a narrow space at the railing with a clear view of the city. I race over to claim it, and Jason stands behind me, since he's tall enough to see over my head.

Lower Manhattan looks majestic. There's no other word I can think of to describe it. People travel from all over the world to see this view right here, and I've got it in my own backyard. If my backyard was a forty-five-minute subway ride away. Still, it's very impressive, and I'm very lucky. All this time, I've been so hung up on escaping Brooklyn and starting over in Silicon Valley, but there's a whole incredible world to discover right here in New York.

This is the city Taylor Swift sings about.

I can see South Street Seaport from here, with its buildings and boats. My mom used to take me there when I was little.

On weekends in the summer, we'd get ice cream cones from Mister Softee, then walk around the pier. I haven't thought about that in a really long time.

The East River below us is inky and calm. In the distance, the Statue of Liberty looks like a tiny spark of light. There are flashes going off around us, people taking selfies and panoramas and posting them to ZigZag. I know I should take a picture, too, but I'm kind of just enjoying being in the moment.

"This is so cool," I say.

"Yeah, the view is awesome from up here." I can feel Jason shift a little behind me. "You know, when you said that sometimes you forget you live in New York City, I figured this would be the perfect place to take you. There's no way you can forget where you live now."

Wow. I am overwhelmed by how much thought he put into this.

"This is the best surprise," I say. "I'm sorry I ever doubted you."

He leans in a little closer, stretching his arms out to grip the railing on either side of me. My gaze drops down from the Manhattan skyline to the backs of his hands. His right thumb extends to stroke the side of my right pinkie, and suddenly I am acutely aware of his presence. His chest presses gently against my back, rising and falling with each breath he takes. His cheek grazes my temple and I inhale sharply and oh damn that cologne is really messing with me.

I try to focus on the reflection of the lights on the water, the sound of the cars rushing past, the chatter of a thousand different tourists. But it's no use. I am completely consumed by Jason Eisler.

My brain must be malfunctioning right now. That must be

why I'm feeling this way. It must also be why I say the most absurd statement in the history of absurd statements.

"This is so romantic, it feels like a date."

"A date?" Jason steps backward so quickly that he bumps into someone behind him. There's a moment of awkward apology followed by a "No worries!" I turn around to make sure everything's okay and there's sweat on his brow.

"I'm just kidding," I say. "It's obviously not a date."

"Obviously," he says. "Like, you and me, on a date? That's completely ridiculous."

Ouch. "Completely."

"I mean, you're with Walker, right?"

"Right. I'm with Walker."

He's scowling now, and I feel like an idiot for even bringing up the word *date* when he's so clearly horrified by the very idea. But honestly, it's all his fault. He's the one who invited me out tonight. He's the one who wore that stupid cologne and put that stupid product in his stupid hair. Plus, he planned this stupidly thoughtful evening. My actual date with Walker was far less romantic than this. No wonder I'm feeling confused.

I'm considering parkouring my way up the arches to escape this awkward situation when New York City comes to the rescue. Plowing toward us through the crowd are a half-dozen people in bright yellow chicken costumes. They're clucking loudly and dropping plastic eggs all over the promenade. Some onlookers are laughing, others are visibly annoyed. As they make their way to the other side of the tower, a man follows closely behind, recording the whole thing on a handheld video camera.

"Wonder if they're gonna post that to their ZigZag channel," I say.

"It's not even funny," Jason says, staring after them with a grimace on his face. "Is that what I look like when I'm pulling pranks?"

"Only if you're wearing a chicken costume."

This gets a laugh out of him, albeit a tiny one. Finally, the spell of awkwardness is broken.

"Think that video will go viral?" he asks.

"Probably not."

We keep walking along the bridge toward Manhattan as though I'd never said that absurd statement. We point out landmarks and crack silly jokes.

Though he's keeping his distance now. He doesn't try to hold my hand, he doesn't even reach for my pinkie. In fact, there's a good six inches of space between us. Maybe even a foot. I can't smell his cologne from here, which is a good thing, in my opinion.

But as I stare out at the New York City skyline, I can't stop thinking about the things Jason and I have in common. We live in the same building, we work at the same store. We love ice cream sundaes and video games. We both like to code. We know how to make each other laugh.

That's a lot. And that's not even everything.

I can't help but wonder if it's the basis for a perfect relationship.

Chapter Fourteen

That night, I have a dream that Walker throws my laptop off the Brooklyn Bridge. I know it's not a premonition or anything. I don't even believe in premonitions. This dream is just my brain's weird way of processing everything that happened during the day. Still, when I wake up, I'm all jittery. Like I can't be sure it didn't actually happen.

I shoot Walker a text: *Hey, what time do you wanna come over to work on your extra credit?* I also type: *You didn't throw my laptop off a bridge, did you?* But I delete that before I hit Send. Even though I'm still kind of wondering if maybe he did.

It's not that I don't *want* to trust Walker. But wanting something won't magically make it happen. For example, I want to believe it was a total coincidence that he and his ex-girlfriend were at the same party the other night. That she was the one hanging all over him and not the other way around. That she really is his ex and not his girlfriend. But I don't know if I do.

Trust doesn't suddenly spring up from wants and wishes. It's built steadily over time. That's why I trust Jason implicitly. In all the years I've known him, he's never given me any reason to doubt the words he says. He's earned my trust.

Of course, the very idea of Jason and I being anything more than friends is completely ridiculous. That's how he described it on the bridge—"completely ridiculous"—after I made that joke about us being on a date. And it was *totally* a joke. I didn't mean it at all. Sure, my mind went to some crazy places at the end of the night, thinking about all the things Jason and I have in common. But it must've been the cologne messing with my head, because the idea of us being in a relationship *is* completely ridiculous.

I'm actually laughing out loud at how ridiculous it is when my phone dings with a text from Walker: *not rly feelin it today.*

Um . . . what?

I text him a string of question marks and he responds with: *not in the mood for math.*

Is one ever really in the mood for math? I'm a Mathlete and even I'm rarely in the mood for math. But Walker's got an extra credit assignment he needs to complete, and Franzen's not going to care that the Muse of Algebra didn't pay him a visit over spring break. Sometimes you've just gotta suck it up and do the stuff you don't want to do.

Also, I really want my laptop back today.

> If you come over right now,
> I'll give you the answers to the next
> five questions in the assignment.

> b there in an hour

I know this solution is not exactly ethical. Walker should be doing his own work. But at the rate we were going yesterday, he'll never finish this assignment in time unless I give him a few more answers.

Also, this seems like the most effective way to get him to bring back my laptop without having an awkward discussion about it.

He arrives an hour later—right on time!—and greets me at the door with another chaste, closed-mouth kiss that leaves my lips buzzing. I'm hugely relieved to see my laptop tucked under his arm, confirming that the image of it sailing into the East River was indeed only a dream.

We sit down at the kitchen table, where I give it a quick once-over to ensure the keyboard and screen and ports are all intact. Looks good! I press the power button and turn to Walker, who's already fidgeting with the edge of the tablecloth.

"Was your dad happy with all the progress we made yesterday?" I ask.

"Yeah, he's off my case now. Thanks a lot for your help."

"No problem. I'm thinking I can get through the next few questions by myself pretty quickly, and then I'll help you work through a couple on your own. If nothing else, you should really get polynomial factoring down. You need to know it for the Regents."

His eyes get this glazed-over look, and I know it's gonna be another afternoon of torture trying to capture his attention long enough to solve an equation. Maybe I'll save us both the agony and do the whole thing for him. If this laptop ever starts up.

Why is this taking so long, anyway? Usually, it boots up quickly, but it's been hanging on the same load screen for several minutes now. There's a little circle spinning in an endless, infuriating loop. I pointlessly jab at some function keys and say, "This is acting weird."

"It was acting weird last night, too," he says.

"Weird how?"

He runs a hand through his perfectly tousled hair. "I was trying to watch a video and all of a sudden the screen went blue. There was some crazy message, I didn't understand what it said. Something about a problem with some file. Then it turned itself off."

Omigod.

What Walker's describing is the "blue screen of death." It's usually caused by hardware malfunctions or errors in low-level software. There's no logical reason this should have happened. Unless Walker did something he wasn't supposed to do.

"What video were you watching?"

He shrugs. "Just some random shit on ZigZag."

I take a deep breath and hold it. Otherwise, I might scream.

Yesterday, when Walker took the laptop, I specifically asked him not to use it for anything except his extra credit assignment. Watching videos on ZigZag was not part of the deal.

Of course, this also means Christine was right. He *does* have a secret ZigZag account. And I'm not important enough for him to tell me about it. I want to ask him why, but right now there are more pressing matters to deal with. Like getting this laptop up and running.

The boot screen finally disappears, and my regular desktop pops up. All the icons are where they're supposed to be. Everything appears normal. The whole thing was probably some weird glitch.

I double-click the file directory to bring up the list of programs. An angry message pops up in the middle of the screen:

```
You're running low on disk space.
```

Um . . . what?

"Did you go to any other websites besides ZigZag?"

"Nah."

"Are you sure?"

He frowns at me, like I'm offending him with this intrusive line of questioning. "Yes, I'm sure."

I jab the Enter key to shut down the dialog box. "Did you click on any strange links or anything?"

"No, I told you. Isaac sent me a video, and when I tried to open it, the computer started acting crazy."

I click on a folder in the file directory labeled "Hackathon Apps." This is where Mr. P installed the code editor, databases, debugging tools, and anything else we could possibly need for the hackathon. But the folder won't open. Instead, another terrifying pop-up message appears:

```
Access denied.
```

This is bad.

"So, you never actually saw any video?"

He shakes his head. "I clicked on it, but then I got that weird blue screen. This stupid laptop couldn't handle it."

Oh no. "The laptop's not the problem, Walker. What you clicked on wasn't a video, it was probably a Trojan horse."

"Nah, it was definitely a video. Isaac said so."

"It was a fake message that tricked you into installing a virus!" I'm having difficulty controlling the sound of my voice. It's suddenly gone from calm and measured to panicky and shrill. "The laptop is completely busted now!"

"Can't you fix it?"

"I have no idea! I told you not to use this for anything except for your math work."

"It was just ZigZag, I didn't think it would be a big deal."

"Well, it is. This laptop doesn't belong to me. It belongs to the school."

"Then it's the school's problem, right?"

"No, it's mine. I had to sign a contract saying I wouldn't loan it out to anyone, and I did and you broke it and I'm gonna have to explain that to Mr. P and he's going to tell my mother and she's going to murder me!" Even worse than getting in trouble with my mom, though? "I can't participate in the hackathon now."

"What's the hackathon?"

He can't be serious. "It's the coding competition I told you about. The highlight of my entire spring break?"

From the blank stare on his face, it clearly doesn't ring a bell. Obviously, he doesn't listen when I speak. Or else he doesn't care enough to commit my words to memory. Either way, it reminds me of my father.

"You don't care about me at all, do you?"

"Calm down." Walker rolls his eyes. "Don't be so dramatic."

"I'm not being dramatic." My voice is wavering, which undermines my claim that I'm not being dramatic, but if you ask me, I think the drama is justified. "This is something that's really important to me and you're treating me like I'm being ridiculous for being upset about it. I trusted you and you totally screwed me over."

"It was an honest mistake. Will you calm down already?"

"Stop telling me to calm down!"

In a flash, he's on his feet, the legs of his chair scraping against the floor. "I'm gonna leave now. I'll come back when you've stopped being such a drama queen."

"You know what? Don't come back at all." This time, there isn't a trace of a waver in my voice.

Walker pauses at the front door with his hand on the knob and turns to look back at me. His hazel eyes shine in the overhead light as he heaves a sigh.

He is so gorgeous.

Then he's gone.

Now I'm alone at the kitchen table, staring at this busted laptop, wondering why I ever put my trust in a guy with a scorpion tattoo.

There must be some way to fix this. I double-click the browser icon, ready to Google up a solution, but any shred of hope I have immediately disintegrates the moment I'm met with the blue screen of death.

This laptop is hosed. No doubt about it.

Mr. P is going to be so disappointed in me. I can't believe I let him down. And how will I ever tell Christine I can't participate in the hackathon? We've been planning this for weeks, and she really wants to win. Plus, I *just* invited Jason to join the team, and now I have to tell him that I'm bailing.

Unless, of course, I can get this laptop fixed.

And it suddenly occurs to me that I know someone who fixes computers for a living. I text Jason: *What time does your dad get home from work today?*

he's working from home.

you wanna hang out with him or something?

I'm having a problem with my school laptop.

I was wondering if you think he could fix it.

dad can fix anything

Is it okay if I come over?

sure. i'm not home now
but i'll txt to tell him you're on your way.

Thank you!

I slap the laptop closed, slip on my shoes, and run down to the fourth floor as fast as I can. Mr. Eisler's already unlocked the door for me and propped it open against the dead bolt. I knock anyway, and he calls out, "Come on in, Ashley!"

Inside, he's sitting in his office. It's actually supposed to be the pantry, but the Eislers cleared out a bunch of shelves and installed a desk so he has his own private work space. When he sees me, he stands up and points to the kitchen table. "Have a seat," he says, and joins me there. "Can I get you something to drink? A snack, maybe?"

"No, thanks." Jason's parents always treat me like a special guest, even though they've known me for basically my entire life.

"Jason tells me you're having an issue with your laptop," he says.

"Yeah." I slide it across the table and he carefully lifts the cover with both hands. As it boots up, ever so slowly, I give an abbreviated version of what went down. "I loaned it to a friend, and I think he installed a virus. He said he clicked on a link to watch some video, but it gave him a blue screen of death. Now

124

my files are locked up and it says the disk space is almost full. Plus, it's taking forever to start up."

"I can see that." When it finishes booting, he nods. "Okay. Let me take a look around and see what I can find."

Mr. Eisler clicks around in silence for a few moments before confirming what I'd already suspected. "You've got a virus, all right. I'm surprised it got past the security scanner. Shouldn't be too bad to fix. I've gotta reboot it in Safe Mode and run a Disk Cleanup. Would you like me to show you how it's done?"

"Yeah, that'd be great." I didn't think anything good could come out of this terrible situation, but for the next hour, Mr. Eisler teaches me a valuable new skill. He walks me through virus removal and shows me how to kill suspicious processes and recover corrupted files. By the time he's done, my laptop is running at full speed, and I'm feeling confident that the next time this happens, I can fix the problem myself. Not that I ever plan on letting there be a next time.

"Thank you so much for fixing this." I stand and hug the laptop to my chest. "And thanks for showing me how to do it."

"It was my pleasure, Ashley. I heard you're doing the hack-athon next weekend?"

"Yeah, I'm super excited for it."

"Jason said you convinced him to sign up." He smiles warmly. "You're such a good influence on him."

"I don't know that it was my influence. He seemed genu-inely interested in it. He's even talking about joining Coding Club."

"Trust me, it's your influence." He pats my shoulder and walks me to the door. "Don't go loaning that laptop out to anyone else, you hear me?"

"Don't worry, I won't."

When I get home, I text Jason: *Your dad fixed it!*

told you he can fix anything

I'm so glad it's working.
I need it for the hackathon!

glad its working too
i need you on my team!

I smile at the thought of being needed and wonder if I really have as much influence over Jason as his dad says I do. Last night, he told me he admires how hard I work. He said I'm the smartest person he knows and that I could be anything I want to be. I should believe in myself as much as he believes in me.

My unfinished hoodie is still sitting on my desk in a pile of wires and fabric and abandoned hope. The last time I worked on this, I was feeling like a failure. I'd let my rejection from ZigZag make me feel like I could never be a software engineer. But now I realize it's just one summer program. It doesn't define my entire future.

I cross the room to pick it up, and as soon as I glance down at the LEDs, it's like there's a spotlight shining on the exact spot I need to rewire. Twenty minutes later, the lights are flashing brightly. Within an hour, I've got them blinking in time to music. It's working. I fixed the problem!

And I've never felt like more of a badass.

Chapter Fifteen

Heaven's leaving for Puerto Rico this weekend, so on Friday, Christine invites us over to her place for a celebratory send-off. It's the last time we'll be able to see Heaven before school's back in session.

Christine told me to come over at two o'clock, so I leave my apartment at 1:40 and take a leisurely springtime stroll to her house on East Fifth Street. By 2:05, I'm on her front stoop ringing the doorbell.

"Hey!" She answers the door with a smile and a hug. "How's it going?"

"Great." I slip off my shoes in the hallway and follow her through her living room toward the basement stairs. Her parents converted their basement into a mini movie theater, with big comfy couches and a projector and everything. It's the perfect place to spend a lazy afternoon. "Is Heaven here yet?"

"No, but she should be here any minute."

It's hard to see, so I descend the steps carefully. Downstairs, the only light is coming from the movie screen, which currently displays the Netflix menu. I wonder if the girls would be up for watching Taylor Swift's documentary again.

As I move toward one of the cream-colored leather recliners, I stop in my tracks. There's a small brown spot on the seat. At first, I think it's one of those peanut-butter-filled pretzel nuggets I like so much. Christine's mom always stocks them in the pantry. But then it trembles the tiniest bit, and I realize it has legs. And antennae.

"Omigod!" I shriek like a banshee and hop backward. My impulse is to run right back up the stairs where I came from, but Christine is blocking my way.

"What is it?" She seems wholly unconcerned that I'm on the verge of an insect-induced panic attack.

"Water bug!"

"Where?"

"There!" I wave my arm frantically in the direction of the recliner. At once, the water bug jerks to life, scurries across the seat, and ducks into the folds of the cushion. "Omigod! It's in the chair!"

I shriek again. Even to my own ear I sound crazed. It's not like my life is in peril. Water bugs are harmless, I know they are. But they're just. So. Gross. I cannot be in the same room with one. Christine and Heaven already know this about me, because a water bug once crawled across our table in Coding Club and I immediately packed up my stuff and left for the day. It's possible I have a minor case of entomophobia—that's fear of insects, I looked it up on the internet—but wouldn't anyone be freaked out by an overgrown cockroach that can run up to three miles an hour?

Christine isn't fazed. "Are you sure? I didn't see anything."

"Yes, I know a water bug when I see one." As if summoned,

it pokes its creepy-crawly antennae out from between the cream-colored cushions. I shriek again, and Christine starts to laugh. "It's not funny!"

"Yes, it is." She walks over to the recliner and picks up the bug between her thumb and forefinger. I cannot believe she's touching this thing. I am so grossed out I want to peel off my skin.

It's resting in the center of her open palm and she's walking toward me with a smile on her face oh god what is wrong with her?

"Get it away from me!" I turn around to run up the stairs, but Heaven's standing on the landing. She's laughing hysterically and has this little remote control in her hand. When she presses a button, the water bug spins in Christine's palm.

Simultaneously, they yell, "April Fool!"

Oh, right. It's April first.

"You guys are cruel." My heart's still racing, and I'm kind of angry, but more than anything, I'm intrigued. "Where did you get that robotic water bug?"

"I made it!" Heaven grabs it from Christine and flips it over to show the hidden mechanism beneath the lifelike exoskeleton. "It was super easy. I slapped a fake bug from the dollar store on top of this miniature motor."

"Cool." I'm still freaked out, but I can't deny that Heaven is an amazing engineer. "How long have you guys been planning this?"

"It was all her idea, I swear!" Christine points at Heaven, who nods in agreement.

"I thought of it a couple of weeks ago," she says.

Funny, I'd forgotten all about April Fools' Day—also known as Jason's favorite day of the year. He always pulls the most epic pranks. Last year, he somehow snuck into the teachers' lounge and filled it with balloons from floor to ceiling. The year before, he glued pennies to the sidewalk on Ocean Parkway and laughed as passersby tried to pick them up. I can't wait to see what he's got planned this year.

Christine and Heaven are still laughing as we curl up on the recliners. There's a full spread of snacks laid out on the coffee table, chips and cookies and Pocky and soda. I drop my phone on the table, then grab a bag of Cheetos and dig in.

"So," Heaven says, popping the top off a can of Pringles. "I've got big news. Shawn asked me to hang out when I get back from Puerto Rico."

"Awesome!" I say.

"Do you know what you guys are gonna do?" Christine asks.

"Well, we've been talking a lot on ZigZag, and it turns out that we're both obsessed with cats but can't get them because our moms are allergic. So we made a reservation at the Brooklyn Cat Cafe. It's ten bucks for a half hour and we can cuddle with as many kitties as we want."

"That sounds fun," I say.

"I can't believe I'm actually going on a date with Shawn Booker." Her smile practically lights up the entire basement.

"That's great." I swear, I'm happy for Heaven. I want to be a supportive friend. But all this talk of ZigZag and dating and making the first move reminds me of everything that happened with Walker. And how badly that all turned out.

Clearly, the girls know where my mind is, because Christine asks, "Did you ever confront Walker about that photo?"

"Yeah. He said it was his ex."

"If it was his ex, then why did he have his arm around her?"

"I mean, he's lying. Obviously." At least, I think he is. Especially since . . . "I found out he has a ZigZag account he's been hiding from me."

"Jerk."

"What's on his profile?" Heaven asks. "Are there any other pictures with that girl?"

"I haven't actually seen his profile." Not for lack of trying. I checked the browser history on my laptop to see if he'd accidentally left himself logged in, but the virus cleanup must've cleared it out.

"Then how did you find out about it?"

I shouldn't have mentioned this. Now I have to admit everything. "I loaned Walker my laptop and he installed a virus on it by clicking some shady ZigZag link." Christine's face goes pale and I quickly follow up with, "Don't worry, it's fixed now."

She looks betrayed. "Ashley, you could've cost us the hackathon."

"I know, I know. It was stupid. But the laptop is fully functional now, and I also know exactly where I stand with Walker. Which is nowhere important."

"So," Heaven asks, "does that mean you guys are broken up?"

"Yeah, I guess." But can you call it a breakup if you aren't entirely sure you were ever in a real relationship?

"Well, it sounds like you're better off without him," Christine says, thoroughly fed up with all this boy talk. "You've got more important stuff to focus on now. They're supposed to announce the judges for the hackathon today and I'm dying to see who it's gonna be."

"Oh, that reminds me," I say. "I asked Jason to join our team and he's in."

Christine frowns. "I hope you're right about him being serious. We don't need him embarrassing us during the competition with some stupid prank."

"Omigod," Heaven says, "his April Fools' Day video is so hilarious this year."

"Oh, he posted it already?" I snatch my phone off the coffee table and pull up his ZigZag channel. "I haven't seen it yet."

"You're gonna die laughing."

Obnoxious music blasts from the phone's speaker as the video starts to play. There's this weird intro sequence with a photo of Jason and a title card that says APRIL FOOLIN' IN BROOKLYN! It reminds me of that video we talked about the other night, the one he said was his top performer. The one Rachel put together for him.

It cuts to an outdoor scene, an area I quickly recognize as the Ocean Parkway Malls. Jason's sitting on a bench, eating a Carvel sundae. Beside him sits his blow-up doll wearing a denim skirtall that buttons up the front. It's actually really cute. I wonder where he got it.

Next, it cuts to a crowded sidewalk, possibly Coney Island Avenue, where he's weaving in and out of a pedestrian intersection while he and his doll engage in some sort of ballroom-dancing routine. Half the people around him look at him like he's crazy; the other half avoid eye contact completely.

In another scene, he's at ShopRite, perusing the produce and asking his doll her opinion on the ripeness of the cantaloupes. In another, he's at the Gravesend Park playground, pushing her on a swing. I'm laughing so hard that my sides are cramping up.

But my laughter comes to an abrupt halt when Rachel appears on the screen. It's only for an instant, and it's not even related to the prank. She just winks at the camera, like she does in her ZigZag videos, before it cuts back to him walking along the street with his doll.

"What's she doing there?" My voice sounds a million miles away.

"Maybe it's a cameo," Christine says. "To help him get more views or something."

"That's stupid."

"It's actually pretty brilliant. Rachel has a ton of followers."

"Are they back together?" Heaven asks.

"I don't know." I close down ZigZag and dim my phone screen. "Why would I know?"

"Uh, I dunno. I figured since you guys are friends." She shoots Christine a look and I quickly realize how snitty I'm being.

"I'm sorry," I say. "I just mean he didn't say anything to me about it, so I'm not sure. I guess it's always possible."

Is it, though? Jason told me Rachel didn't understand him. That she wanted him to be someone he's not. So why would she be back in the picture now?

My phone buzzes in my hand and the screen lights up with an email notification. Christine's phone buzzes, too, and she glances down, Heaven peering over her shoulder. I tap it twice to open the message, grateful for the distraction from Jason and Rachel, and nearly choke when I read what it says:

Announcing the Latest Sponsors of the NYC High School Hackathon: ZigZag!

The New York City High School Spring Break Hackathon is proud to announce a last-minute surprise partnership with

133

ZigZag, makers of the most popular social media platform in the United States. The technical challenge provided on the day of the hackathon will involve the ZigZag platform—so be sure you familiarize yourself with the app beforehand!

ZigZag will be providing food, beverages, and swag for all hackathon participants, as well as a judging panel consisting of ZigZag employees from their software engineering, product development, and media partnership departments.

In addition to the prizes previously announced, the judges will be awarding an additional prize to the first-place team: a summer internship at ZigZag headquarters in Silicon Valley.

Christine and Heaven squeal at the same time that I shriek, louder than I did when I was being terrorized by that robotic water bug. Because this is far more shocking. And far more significant.

ZigZag rejected me from their internship program, but all they knew of me was what was printed on my transcript. This is my chance to show them firsthand exactly who I am and what I'm capable of. To prove I'm more than some letters and numbers on a piece of paper.

My stomach twists and clenches. There's no way I can lose out on this opportunity a second time.

"We have to win first place," I say. "We have to."

"We will," Christine says.

"Dang." Heaven sighs. "Now I really wish I was going to the hackathon."

Chapter Sixteen

What was supposed to be a celebratory send-off turns into a marathon research-and-planning session. Since the hackathon challenge will revolve around ZigZag, Christine and I need to learn everything we can about the app and how it's built. So instead of stuffing our faces and watching TV, Heaven helps us put together a study and practice schedule for the hackathon, outlining all the ZigZag-specific technology we should brush up on before the big day.

For example, ZigZag uses its own proprietary programming language to code their app. I learned a little bit about it while I was putting together my application for the summer internship, but if I want to knock those judges' socks off, I need to become an expert. And even though we all have ZigZag accounts, there are a lot of features we haven't explored, like advertising and photo editing. When we walk into that room next Friday morning, we need to know the product inside and out.

This means hours of research, experimenting, and investigation. Aside from my weekend shift at ShopRite, all I'll be doing for the next seven days is living and breathing ZigZag.

I'm still studying at midnight, huddled in bed with my laptop, when my phone dings with a text from Dad: *Sorry honey, can't make it for breakfast tomorrow morning. Got a lot of packing to do for the Bahamas!*

I knew this was coming. Of course I did. Yet for some reason, I'm still disappointed. You'd think by now I'd be immune to being disappointed by my father, but it's like there's some tiny little girl living inside my brain who desperately wants to believe he will change. Every weekend, against my will, she whispers, "Maybe he'll show up this time!" But, most of the time, he doesn't. And then I'm left feeling angry and resentful.

In an ideal world, my dad and I would have the kind of relationship where we talk about feelings. Then I'd be able to tell him all about how his constant flaking disappoints me, or how his clear preference for Stefanie's kids is deeply, deeply hurtful. But the truth is, my dad doesn't care. He's unreliable and emotionally unavailable, and he will never, ever change.

I text Jason: *Dad bailed on breakfast. Walk to work in the morning?* and he replies with a 👍. I wonder where he is right now. If he's with Rachel. If they're really back together or if it was just some publicity stunt to increase his chances of going viral. I go to his ZigZag channel to check on his stats and find he's already got more than a thousand views on his "April Foolin' in Brooklyn!" video. That's huge, considering it's been up for less than twenty-four hours. Rachel really *does* know what she's doing.

As I watch the video for the second time, I try to block out the obnoxious background music and crazy graphics so I can focus on the most entertaining part: Jason clowning around and being his natural, hilarious self. He cavorts on the playground, and I can't contain my laughter. He dances down the street, and warmth spreads through the center of my chest.

Then Rachel appears in the frame, winking seductively, and the warmth is replaced with a cold, empty space. I shut down the app and toss my phone aside.

Whatever's going on with Jason and Rachel is none of my business. Still, the thought of them being together keeps me tossing and turning until dawn. When my alarm goes off at eight o'clock, I feel like I haven't slept a wink. I get dressed in a fog, scarf down breakfast, and head to the fourth floor to knock on Jason's door. I'm a few minutes early, and Jason usually runs a few minutes late, so I'm fully expecting one of his parents to answer the door. But instead it's him, fully dressed and ready to go.

"You're on time," I say, unable to hide my surprise.

"Actually, I'm early." He walks toward the elevator and jams the Down button with his thumb. "Impressed?"

"Maybe. What gives?"

"I dunno. Just woke up in a good mood. Feel like I have a lot of energy."

Before I can inquire about the source of his good mood, the elevator door rumbles open. Mrs. Finkel is standing inside, squinting at the floor numbers like she's never seen them before.

"Have you seen this?" She gestures to the prank sticker Jason slapped up there more than a week ago. I can't believe the super hasn't taken it down yet.

"It says the elevator's voice-activated now." Her voice is thin and raspy with age. "Been up for a while, but I can't get it to work. Can you? Maybe I'm not talking loud enough." She inches forward so her mouth is nearly touching the emergency speaker and she screeches, "Lobby!"

Poor Mrs. Finkel. It's hard not to feel bad for her as she stands there screaming pointlessly at the wall. It's also hard not to laugh.

Jason doesn't even crack a smile, though. "You know, I don't think it's working, Mrs. Finkel. I'll ask my parents to talk to the super about it."

She grunts disapprovingly. "Nothing works the way it's supposed to these days. All this technology that's supposed to make our lives better. You know what I say? No thank you. Give me an old-fashioned phone with a cord."

The door closes and we ride down to the lobby together. The whole time, Mrs. Finkel grouses about smartphones and the evils of technology, and I stare at my feet to avoid breaking out in hysterical laughter.

We let Mrs. Finkel exit the elevator first and follow along behind her. As he's leaving, I see Jason scratch at the edge of the sticker before peeling it off in one sheet.

When we're out on Bay Parkway, I ask, "Why are you in such a good mood?"

He smiles wide. "I posted a video for April Fools' Day and it set a new record for most views on my channel. Did you see it?"

"Yeah. It was great." That's all I say. I can't bring myself to comment on how funny it was or how much I laughed, because then I'd be praising Rachel, the girl who wants him to be someone he's not. Instead, I change the subject. "Did you get that email about the hackathon?"

He clears his throat. "Uh, yeah. ZigZag's sponsoring it now, huh?"

"Yup. And first prize is now an internship at their headquarters in Silicon Valley."

"I thought of you when I saw that. How it's kind of like your second chance."

"That's why we need to win. Christine and I came up with this study and practice plan to make sure we know everything about ZigZag's technology beforehand. How it works, what people use it for, stuff like that. It would really be helpful if you got in on it, too."

"Of course. Anything you need. I mean, you deserve to win more than anybody."

I'm getting that squirmy feeling in my stomach again, the same one I got the night we were on the Brooklyn Bridge. But there's no product in his hair and he's not wearing that pomander-scented cologne—which I hate now, by the way—so I'm not sure what's going on.

"Do you think it might help if we had another team member?" he asks. "We can have up to four. You said the more brainpower, the better, right?"

"Right," I say. "But I don't know anyone else who'd be interested. Especially on such short notice."

"I know someone."

"Who?"

"Rachel Gibbons."

My stomach stops squirming and bottoms out. "What makes you think she'd be interested in the hackathon?"

"She told me. When she found out ZigZag was gonna be giving away swag, she was all about it. You know her: she loves ZigZag."

He can't be serious. "Great, she loves ZigZag, so does every teenager in the country. But does she know how to code? Because that's what's really important here."

"Not that I know of, but you told me you don't need to be a strong coder to participate. Besides, she knows way more about how ZigZag works and what people use it for than you or me or Christine. She could help us come up with original ideas for the challenge. She's great with that stuff. Look at what she does for my videos."

He's got an awful lot of good things to say about her. "Are you guys back together or something?"

"What does it matter to you?"

"Well, the other night you were saying how little you had in common and how you were doomed from the very beginning. It just . . . it seems a little weird."

"Weirder things have happened."

"Like what?"

"Like you and Beech." He scowls. "No breakfast date this morning, huh?"

"Shut up," I say, but it doesn't sound like I mean it.

"Get any more tattoos lately?"

I don't even dignify that with a response.

"Was he the one who jacked up your laptop?"

This catches me off guard. I didn't mention Walker's name to Mr. Eisler. "How did you know it was him?"

"Educated guess. He's the only person I could think of who you knew who would be stupid enough to install a virus."

"Will you shut up?" This time, I sound like I mean it. "He's not stupid. It was an honest mistake."

"Sorry. Didn't mean to insult your boyfriend." His voice is dripping with sarcasm, and I'm furious with him for acting so superior. I'm also furious with myself for jumping to Walker's defense. It's not like he deserves it.

But I'm not about to give Jason the satisfaction of knowing Walker and I are through. He's been ragging on him from the second he found out we were together. It's like he couldn't even be happy for me. And now he's inexplicably dating Rachel again and rubbing the whole thing in my face, as if he didn't spend the other night telling me all about how they were so wrong for each other.

Whatever. If Jason wants to be with a girl who doesn't appreciate him for who he is, that's his prerogative.

For the rest of the walk, we don't speak. I pick up the pace, always staying half a step ahead of him, and when we get to the store, I race to the staff room to change into my vest. All the while, I can feel Jason staring at me, but I refuse to look his way. If we make eye contact, I may scream. Either that or burst into tears. Because even though I know the idea of us being in a relationship is completely ridiculous, it hurts me to think about him being in a relationship with Rachel.

Or with anyone else, for that matter.

So to be safe, I head to the cash registers with my eyes on the ground, then lose myself in my work so I don't have to think about the way I feel.

Chapter Seventeen

I don't walk home with Jason. In fact, I duck out of work five minutes early to avoid running into him in the staff room. I'm not mad at him or anything, I just don't want to talk to him right now, because then I'll start feeling feelings. Squirmy, uncomfortable, messy feelings that interfere with my ability to concentrate. And I've got plans this evening that require my full concentration.

According to my hackathon study and practice schedule, tonight I'm supposed to review ZigZag's application programming interface, or API for short. The API is a really powerful tool that lets you hook into ZigZag's database to get user statistics, like how quickly someone grew their following or how many times their profile has been viewed. It's super interesting, and I bet it'll come in handy during the hackathon.

I'm playing around with the messaging feature when Mom knocks on my bedroom door. "You have a visitor," she says. "Jason's here. Can I let him in?"

So much for my concentration.

"Sure," I say, setting aside my laptop and smoothing my hands over my hair. I should've showered after work, or at least changed my clothes. Though I'm not sure why I suddenly care about my appearance. Jason's seen me looking way worse than this.

When he walks through the door, I get that squirmy feeling in my stomach.

"Hey," he says, casual as ever, before plopping down on my bed right next to me. I slide over to put some space between us, which he notices right away. "You still mad at me?"

"I'm not mad."

"You avoided me all day and cut out early without telling me."

"I had to get home. I'm studying for the hackathon."

He glances at my laptop, then back at me. "I'm sorry about what I said before."

"It's fine."

"No, it isn't. Look, I don't like Beech, but if he's good to you, that's all that matters. I'm sorry I keep making you feel bad about it."

"Why don't you like him?"

"I've heard things." I gesture for him to elaborate, and he grimaces, like he's swallowed something sour. "He's a player, all right? He hooks up with a lot of girls."

Instantly, I think of the picture of Walker at that party, with his arm around that beautiful girl. The explanation he gave me sounded plausible—it was his ex, she was drunk, he didn't want to cause any drama—but I'll bet anything it was a lie.

"Anyway," Jason continues, "it's your life. I just think he's trouble. And you can do better."

This statement offends me, even though I sort of agree. I frown and fold my arms across my chest. "Well, I think you can do better, too."

He gets that sour look again, and for a split second, I'm afraid he's going to get up and leave. Then his face suddenly softens, and he says, "I didn't come here to argue with you, okay? I came here to show you this."

He pulls his phone from his pocket and starts tapping away at the screen. If he shows me another video with a cameo from Rachel, I swear I'm going to throw up.

Thankfully, it turns out to be another app he's coded. "I've been working on this over the past few days. It's my spin on the Magic 8 Ball." He hands me the phone. There's a big blue question mark on the screen. "Ask it a question, then give it a shake."

There are about a dozen different questions floating through my brain: Did Walker ever actually like me? Is Jason happy now that he's back with Rachel? Will this squirmy feeling in my stomach ever go away?

But the only one I'm not afraid to say out loud is, "Will our team win the hackathon?"

I shake the phone and the question mark turns into a bright blue swirl. Then a bell sounds, and the answer appears: ALL SIGNS POINT TO YES.

"This is really cool," I say, handing the phone back to him.

"You've done cooler. Speaking of which, how's your hoodie coming along?"

"I finished it! There are still some tweaks I want to make in terms of color and brightness, but I've got the lights blinking in time to music now."

"Cool! Can I see it in action?"

"Sure." It's hanging in my armoire for safekeeping—after all that work I put in, there's no way I want to risk it getting damaged—so I get up, cross the room, and grab it off the hanger. Carefully, I slip it on over my T-shirt and zip it up to my chin, and as I press the button to turn it on, my chest swells with pride for my accomplishment. There were so many times I wanted to give up on this project, but I didn't. Instead, I kept at it, trying over and over and over again until I found the solution to my problem. Just like a real, badass software engineer.

In this hoodie, I feel like a glowing ray of light. The LEDs lining the edges of the zipper, cuffs, and hood are bright and brilliant, and Jason's looking at me like I'm some kind of superstar. I know he's just mesmerized by the lights in the hoodie, but for a moment, I imagine he's mesmerized by me.

"Kill the lights." His voice is softer than I've ever heard it. "I wanna get the full effect."

Heat rushes to my cheeks. Jason leans back and the sight of him reclining against my pillow has rendered me incapacitated. It takes a great deal of effort to reach over and turn off the lamp, but when I do, the room goes dark and my body glows even brighter. The LEDs reflect in his chocolate-brown eyes and I'm suddenly finding it very hard to breathe.

"They blink?" he asks.

"When there's music," I say.

"Hold on." He picks up his phone and scrolls through it with his thumb. A few taps and the opening drumbeat of "Lover" fills the room. Soon Taylor Swift is singing about dazzling haze and mysterious ways and the lights framing my face dance along to the rhythm of her voice.

Of course Jason would choose this song. He knows it's the title track to my favorite Taylor Swift album. When it first came out, I played it on repeat for hours. He listened to me warble every word and analyze the meaning of every lyric, and not once did he complain about it or make fun of me.

I can't imagine Walker ever caring that much about the things I care about. He doesn't even listen when I talk.

But Jason? Jason cares. And he knows everything there is to know about me, from my greatest hopes to my deepest fears. He even knows my favorite flavor of Mentos. Plus, he's funny and thoughtful and encourages me to succeed, even when I feel like I'm a total failure. He likes me for who I am, and not for who he thinks I should be. He believes in me.

I think I might be in love with him.

Without warning, my bedroom door flies open. Mom announces, "I made chicken cutlets for dinner if you're—" Then she cuts herself off when she discerns the darkness, the flashing lights, the slow smoky vocals of Taylor Swift. She looks from me to Jason and back again, then clears her throat. "Jason, you're welcome to stay for dinner," she says, then closes the door.

Jason stops the music. I flip on the lights and turn off my hoodie. The moment is over.

"I should get home." He hops off my bed and pockets his phone. "My mom's probably getting dinner on the table, too."

"Right."

We avoid looking at each other as we walk to the front door. "See you later," he says, then calls to my mother in the kitchen, "See you later!"

"Bye, Jason," she calls, and then he's gone.

Mom's gonna want to talk about this, I know it. Maybe if I slip into my seat and start shoveling food into my mouth immediately, she'll get the hint and ignore what she just saw in there. Which wasn't much of anything, I guess, except for whatever was going on inside my head. Like the realization that I'm in love with Jason Eisler.

146

Unfortunately, my plan doesn't work. "So, what was going on in there?" she asks.

Through a mouthful of broccoli, I say, "I was showing Jason my Coding Club project."

"Mm." She takes a bite of her chicken cutlet and swallows. "What happened with the boy you went out with last week? Walker?"

She stares at me and the back of my neck starts to throb. I know Mom can't see the tattoo with my hair down like this, but I still live in fear of her finding it.

"We broke up," I say.

"Oh, I'm sorry." She doesn't sound like she's actually sorry. "What happened?"

It's such a simple question, but the answer is complicated, and I don't feel like getting into the details of how and why Walker and I were doomed from the start. But I'm still mad at the way he treated me, so I say, "He's a liar."

"Good riddance, then. There's nothing worse than a liar." She takes another bite of her chicken cutlet. "What about Jason?"

"What *about* Jason?"

She shrugs one shoulder. "You two seem like a good match. I mean, you have so much in common."

I don't disagree. We have the basis for the perfect relationship, don't we? The problem is he's with Rachel now, so . . . "It's not gonna happen. He doesn't like me like that."

Mom's silent for a minute. She takes a few bites of chicken, a sip of water. Then she says, "I wouldn't be so sure about that."

Chapter Eighteen

When I was studying for the SAT, I would memorize key vocabulary words by repeating the definitions over and over again in my head. While waiting at the bus stop or bagging groceries, I'd silently review the meanings of words like *austere* and *pragmatic* and *repudiate*. Eventually, I could recite them without effort. Words like *vernacular* became part of my vernacular, and my vocabulary exploded.

That's because repetition is the key to remembering. And I figure I could use this same tactic to remember something very important that I seem to have forgotten.

Namely, that I am not in love with Jason Eisler.

For the rest of the night, I silently chant those eight words in my head, and by the next morning, I think I'm finally cured. When I swing by Jason's apartment before we walk to work, there's the tiniest ache in my chest the moment he opens the door and I catch sight of his face. But after a dozen or so silent repetitions of my mantra, the ache goes away.

Because I am not in love with Jason Eisler.

I can't get Mom's words out of my head, either. I'm sure she's wrong, but still. Maybe she knows something I don't. Maybe this is one of those things she and Mrs. Eisler talk about when they get together for coffee or something. It's hard to imagine Jason confiding in his mother about his true feelings for me, but he probably doesn't have to say anything to her at all. Moms sometimes have this sixth sense about things. Like they know how you're feeling before you're even aware you're feeling it.

Anyway, it doesn't matter. Because Jason's back together with Rachel Gibbons. Even if I was in love with him—which I'm *not*—he's already spoken for. The best thing I can do is pretend I never had those feelings in the first place.

A great way to get my mind off of those pesky feelings? Work. After clocking eight hours at ShopRite, I head home and continue to lose myself in hackathon prep. Tonight, I'm reviewing ZigZag's advertising platform, which seems to be the way they make most of their money.

As I'm going over all the different types of ad offerings, my phone dings with a text from Walker.

> wut r u doin wensday nite?
> can u hang?

No *Hi* or *How are you?* or *Sorry I'm a thoughtless jerk who broke your laptop.* Just a painfully misspelled question about what I'm doing three days from now. After the way we left things, you'd think he'd have the decency to show a little remorse. But of course he doesn't. Because he doesn't care about me.

I type *You're a jerk,* then delete it. I type *Screw you,* then delete that, too. What I really want to type is, *Did you ever actually like me, or was I just some girl you were trying to play?* Instead, I type *I'm busy that night.*

But before I can hit Send, another message arrives. This time, an image of a QR code and some words that are too small to read. I tap it, zoom in, and the air rushes out of my lungs.

These are concert tickets. Two of them, to be precise.

Wednesday, eight p.m. At the Barclays Center in Brooklyn.

Taylor Swift on tour.

Is this real? I write back.

yah, he responds. *i rly wanted to make it up to u. im sorry for wut i did with ur laptop. and for calling u a drama queen. ur not a drama queen. u had evry rite to be mad.*

Wow. This seems like a sincere apology. He understands what he did wrong and why I was upset. Maybe he *does* care about me after all.

I'm so astonished by this revelation, I can't think of the proper words to respond. I'm staring at my phone, completely dumbfounded, when he sends another text: *is this ok?*

Is this *okay?* This is more than okay. This is amazing. And kind of unbelievable.

> Of course!
> This is incredible!
> How did you even get the tickets?
> They've been sold out for months!

> don't worry about it 😌

Omigod. I can't believe this. I'm going to see Taylor Swift live!

> Thank you thank you!
> I can't wait! ☺

me neither 🖤

At the sight of that tiny digital heart, I let loose with a squeal so high-pitched I'm shocked my phone screen doesn't crack into a thousand pieces.

All this time, I thought Walker wasn't listening when I spoke, but I couldn't have been more wrong. He remembered that I wanted to go to this concert. And he must've paid an absurd amount of money to get these tickets. How could he even afford them?

I guess it just goes to show how much he really likes me. Sure, he's made mistakes—big, awful mistakes—but he acknowledged them and now he's trying to make things right. Maybe Walker and I weren't actually doomed from the start. And if Jason gave Rachel a second chance, maybe I should give Walker a second chance, too.

Mom materializes in my doorway, her brow etched with concern despite the wide smile on my face. "Everything okay in here? I thought I heard you screaming."

My head is spinning and it's hard to parse my thoughts. I blurt out, "Can I go to the Taylor Swift concert on Wednesday? I'd have to be out past curfew, but it's spring break. I don't have classes or work the next day or anything. It's at Barclays, so I won't even have to leave Brooklyn." She narrows her eyes, so I urge her, "Mom, please, it's Taylor Swift. This is, like, a once-in-a-lifetime opportunity."

"Who are you going with?"

The spinning in my head comes to an abrupt and jerky halt.

I can't tell her I'm going with Walker. I already told her he was a liar. If I backpedal now, she'll have a million and one questions, and if I give the wrong answer, she'll tell me I can't go.

Nothing can jeopardize this night. I know it's wrong to lie to my mom, but these are truly extraordinary circumstances. I mean, Taylor Swift.

"Christine," I say. "She won tickets through a contest on ZigZag."

Mom's eyes get narrower and she purses her lips. She must know I'm lying. I'll bet she knows all about the tattoo on the back of my neck, too. I steel myself for an epic scolding, but all she does is nod. "Okay. Just be careful. And keep your phone on the whole time."

"Of course!" As she turns to leave, I say, "Thanks so much, Mom."

"You're welcome." She turns back to look at me, her eyes suddenly warm and soft, like a hug. "You work so hard. You deserve to have a little fun."

After she walks away, I sit there and stare at the empty space she left behind, thinking about how easily that lie slipped out of my mouth. I didn't have to think about what to say or how to say it. It's like it came to me fully formed. Her words from last night echo in my mind: *There's nothing worse than a liar.*

But who am I really hurting with this lie? No one. Walker made a mistake and he apologized. I'll explain all that to Mom later on, after the concert, when we're officially back together. Then I'll have Walker come over to meet her, and she can see for herself that he's not such a bad guy.

For now, though, I'm not going to waste my time feeling guilty or ashamed. Because this is a time for celebration.

I'm going to see Taylor Swift!

Chapter Nineteen

I spend the next three days hunkered down in my room with my laptop, preparing for the hackathon. Sometimes I feel like there's so much to learn, my brain isn't big enough to absorb it all.

I also spend a lot of time scrolling through ZigZag for the latest Taylor Swift concert news. Apparently, she's been switching up her setlist from city to city, so every show is unique. This performance at Barclays is going to be a complete surprise. I can't remember ever feeling this excited about anything.

And I'm not only excited about seeing Taylor. I'm also excited about seeing Walker. Tonight will be a brand-new start for us. Like hitting the factory reset button on a malfunctioning device.

It takes me forever to get ready. I change clothes four times before settling on my usual outfit of T-shirt, jeans, and Converse. Then I top it off with my paper airplane necklace—for good luck!—and zip into my light-up hoodie.

As I'm heading out the door, I tell Mom, "I'm meeting Christine at the subway station."

"Come home as soon as the concert's over," she says. "And don't make eye contact with anyone on the train."

"I know, Mom." It's like she thinks I'm still a child with no concept of situational awareness. I resist the urge to roll my eyes and give her a quick kiss on the cheek before heading out the door.

Walker's waiting for me outside the station. He's leaning back against the brick wall, staring down at his phone. Probably scrolling through ZigZag.

I tap him on the shoulder and give a little wave. He instantly dims his phone screen and smiles. "Hey."

"Hey."

He leans in for a kiss—no doubt another chaste peck on the lips—but instead of meeting him halfway, I take a step back. It's his cologne. It transports me to last week, when I was on the Brooklyn Bridge, holding hands with Jason as we gazed out over the East River. This scent is now forever linked to that moment in time.

Walker gives me a weird look, and then we're both distracted by the rumble and clack of an approaching train. We race down the stairs to catch it, then let it whisk us away to downtown Brooklyn.

There's an empty two-seater we claim as our own. Walker leans forward, elbows on knees, fidgeting with a hole in his jeans, while I sit back and stare at the floor. The train passes station after station. People get on, people get off. The recorded voice tells us to stand clear of the closing doors. We're halfway to our destination already, and Walker and I haven't said a single word to each other aside from "Hey."

We don't have anything to talk about. I already knew this.

We have nothing in common. Still, we should be able to hold a conversation, right?

I start with a softball question. "Are you excited for the concert?"

He shrugs. "Yeah, I guess."

"You *guess*?" I can't hide my horror.

"I mean, I'm happy to go. It's just . . . I'm not the biggest Taylor Swift fan."

"Oh." Suddenly, I feel really guilty. A couple weeks ago, I checked StubHub to see if there were any reasonably priced tickets for tonight's show. The cheapest one was more than four hundred dollars, and it had a partially obstructed view of the stage. Walker must feel really bad about this whole laptop debacle if he was willing to spend that much money to see a show when he doesn't even like the artist. Unless he had some sort of hookup or something.

"How did you get these tickets?"

His mouth twists into a smirk, like he's about to tell me again not to worry about it. But before he can, I say, "No, really. How did you get them?"

He shifts in his seat. "My mom's boyfriend. He's a ticket broker. I told him about what happened, with the laptop and you and my dad and stuff. So he called in a favor and got these for me. Anything to make my mom happy, you know?"

Actually, I don't know. Most of what he said doesn't even make sense. I start with the most pressing question at hand. "What's a ticket broker?"

"He buys tickets in bulk for all kinds of events. Broadway shows, basketball games, concerts. Then he resells them for a higher price. Makes a fortune."

"Isn't that illegal?"

"Nah. He says there's rules about what you can and can't do, but as long as your business looks aboveboard, you're good."

I always wondered how it was possible for tickets to sell out so fast, only to immediately be made available on another website for jacked-up prices. This explains it. Even if it's legal, it still seems unfair. Then again, I *am* benefiting from it right now.

"Well, thanks again. This is like a dream come true for me. I've been a huge fan ever since *1989*."

"What?" He pulls a face like I've told him something inconceivable. "How old are you?"

I can't help but laugh. "Not the year 1989. *1989* is the name of her fifth album. It was actually released in 2014. I'm sure you've heard some of the songs on there. I mean, 'Shake It Off' is one of her biggest hits. You know that one, right?"

"I think so, yeah." His eyes are starting to get that glazed look, but I plod on. I can talk about Taylor's oeuvre for hours. Plus, it's not like he's coming up with some other interesting topic of conversation.

"Anyway, I loved it when I first heard it, but I was still too young to really understand the meaning behind her lyrics, you know? She really puts herself out there in such an emotional, vulnerable way. All of her feelings and experiences she has in her relationships, she pours it all into her songs. If you listen to *Lover* from start to finish, you can almost . . ." I trail off when Walker starts snickering. "What?"

"Nothing." He's smiling, but it's not a nice smile. It almost feels like he's making fun of me.

"No, what are you laughing at?"

"You put a lot of thought into what Taylor Swift is writing about."

"I told you, I'm a big fan."

"You sound more like you're obsessed."

"I'm not obsessed. I just really love her music and admire her as a person. I feel like she understands me in a way that no one else does."

"That's crazy." He lets out a big laugh. "She has no idea who you are."

"That's not what I mean." My voice sounds small. There's no way I can possibly explain this to him, because he obviously doesn't want to understand it. I feel sorry for him, in a way. That he doesn't know what it's like to be part of a fandom, to feel connected to people you don't even know because of artwork that speaks to your soul.

He's still laughing, oblivious to my feelings. I thought he was bringing me to this concert to make me feel better. Not to make me feel stupid for liking what I like.

Jason never makes fun of my love for Taylor Swift. I don't know if he actually cares about the secret meaning I extract from her lyrics, but at least he pretends to. Because he knows how important it is to me.

Walker finally stops laughing, and we don't speak for the rest of the ride. As the train gets closer to Barclays, the car gets more crowded. By the time we pull into the Atlantic Avenue station, it's standing room only. The doors open and we follow the wave of people onto the platform and up the stairs.

Walker holds my hand as we pass through security and navigate our way around the expansive lobby. Anyone watching us would think we were a carefree teenage couple enjoying a night out on spring break. They can't see the doubt and dread taking up space in my brain.

I know I should be overjoyed. I'm on my way to the concert

of my dreams with the boy I've been crushing on for the better part of a year. But it's suddenly occurred to me that getting back together with Walker won't be as simple as hitting a factory reset button. There's still so much we don't know about each other. So much we don't understand, so little we have in common. Not to mention the unanswered questions: Who was that girl in the photo? What's up with his secret ZigZag profile? We may be dealing with something worse than a minor malfunction, worse even than a blue screen of death. We may be completely unsalvageable.

Once we enter the arena, though, any concerns I have about the state of my relationship with Walker float away into the rafters. These seats are *good*. Lower level, not too far back, and with a central view of the stage. Any minute, Taylor's going to walk out and light the place on fire. I touch my paper airplane necklace and think that maybe every bad thing that happened over the last couple of weeks was worth it, just to be here.

I'm buzzing with nervous energy, so much so that when Walker squeezes my hand, I squeal. "This is so cool!"

"I'm glad you like it." He reaches out and pulls me in for a hug. I hug him back, but I can't tear my eyes away from the stage. There are three huge screens and a runway that bisects the general admission pit. I wonder if she'll have pyrotechnics. Can they even set off fireworks indoors?

This hug is lasting an awfully long time. And Walker's hands are starting to wander. Over my shoulder blades, down my spine. He buries his face in the crook of my neck and his breath is hot on my skin and this all feels too far and too fast.

I wriggle away, smiling so he doesn't get offended. "This is so cool!" I say the same stupid thing again, because I need to fill the silence.

He smiles, but it's not very convincing. "I'm gonna go to the concession stands. Do you want anything?"

"Yeah. Um . . ." We passed by so many food stalls when we walked through the main concourse. There were tacos and chili dogs and ice cream sundaes. I can't decide, so I say, "Surprise me!" Then I hold my breath until he walks away.

This is weird. I never would've thought a hug from Walker Beech would make me feel uncomfortable, but it just felt wrong. I refuse to let boy problems ruin my night, though. Like Taylor, I shake it off and turn my attention back to the stage. It looks so pristine, I should take a picture before it gets covered in confetti and firework ash.

I pull my phone from my pocket and find five texts from Mom.

I see you made it to Barclays.

Have a great time!

Are you okay?

Why aren't you answering me???

Don't make me regret letting you go!

When I was younger, I couldn't wait until I got my own phone. To me, it symbolized adulthood and independence and freedom. Little did I know it would turn my mom into a low-key stalker.

I snap a selfie with the stage in the background and send it to her with the message, *Sorry! Was so caught up in this amazingness I forgot to check my phone!*

She replies instantly. *Tell Christine I said hi.* 💙

I am the worst, most dishonest daughter in the universe.

A few minutes later, Walker returns with two enormous

plastic cups, liquid sloshing over the brims. No food, but I can't really be upset about that. I told him to surprise me, after all. I probably should've been more specific. Surprise me with *food*.

He's got a sly smile on his face as he hands me my drink, then tips his cup in my direction and says, "Cheers."

I put my lips to the edge and immediately recoil. This drink smells funny. Strong and sour, kind of like a rotten apple. "Is this beer?"

"Yeah. Do you not like Bud Light?"

"Uh . . ." I don't want to admit that I've never had a Bud Light. Or any other type of beer, for that matter. "No, it's okay. How did you get this?"

He dips his head down and mutters, "Fake ID."

"Oh." I don't mean to be ungrateful. He probably thinks I like beer. But I'm not about to get drunk for the first time at a Taylor Swift show. Tonight, I want to be fully present, and tomorrow, I want to remember every detail. So I say, "Thanks," then fake a sip and stick it in the cupholder. I don't plan on touching it again.

Moments later, the house lights dim. Screeches erupt around the arena, echoing off the ceiling and filling the cavernous space with a power and spark that only nineteen thousand Swifties can muster. A drumbeat pulses through the sound system. My heart beats in time. I can sense the blood rushing through my veins, the screams reverberating off my eardrums. There's magic in this room, I can feel it.

I reach inside my hoodie and flip a switch. Instantly, the LEDs glow pink and purple and blue. As the music swells, they keep rhythm. It almost feels like I'm part of the show.

Someone taps me on the shoulder. I turn around and in the

row behind me, there's a group of girls smiling. One of them yells, "I love your hoodie!"

"Thanks!" I yell back.

"Where'd you get it? I want one!"

"I made it!"

Their mouths fall open, and one of them yells, "No way! You are so freakin cool!"

My cheeks ache from the strain of smiling so wide. When I was making this hoodie, I didn't expect anyone to think I was cool. I made it because it was fun and challenging. It felt good to create something using my brain and my own two hands. "Cool" wasn't something that ever factored in.

I have to admit, though: it feels damn good to have this total stranger tell me I'm cool.

I glance over at Walker, to see his reaction. But he's not reacting. He's not even paying attention. His nose is buried in his phone, his thumbs are tapping away.

He doesn't see my hoodie. He doesn't see me.

The last time I wore this hoodie, Jason couldn't take his eyes off me.

Like I said, I don't mean to be ungrateful. This night is magical, no doubt. But it's not perfect. The only way it could be perfect is if Jason were here.

Chapter Twenty

Perfect or not, the concert is incredible.

Once Taylor takes the stage, nothing else matters. Her moves are graceful, her voice is flawless. When she strums "You Belong with Me" on her guitar, I sing along to every word. When she plays "Lover" on her rhinestone-encrusted piano, I nearly break down in tears. There's only one word to describe the experience: *transcendent.* I feel connected to everyone in the arena, while at the same time feeling like I'm the only person on Earth.

Actually, there's one person in the arena who I'm definitely not feeling connected to. Walker's been scrolling through his phone nonstop since the opening number, pausing only to chug his beer. When he finishes his, he proceeds to drink mine, and then goes off to the concession stands to buy himself a third.

Whatever. If he wants to get wasted during the greatest show in history, that's his prerogative.

The problem is, he's getting sort of sloppy. Not falling-down drunk or anything, but there's a definite sway to his stance. At one point, he sloshes beer onto my sneaker. He doesn't apologize, but I don't think he's even aware that it happened.

When Taylor launches into "I Forgot That You Existed," I decide to take her advice and forget all about Walker's existence. I dance to the music, and so do the lights on my hoodie. Halfway through the song, Walker grabs me by the waist and says, "I'm gonna hit the bathroom."

I turn to watch him wobble away. As he waits for the girl next to him to step aside and let him pass, he tries to slip his phone into his back pocket. It catches the very edge of the fabric, then clatters to the floor. He must be too drunk to realize what he's done, because he doesn't bend down to retrieve it. He just disappears down the aisle and into the darkness.

I pick up the phone before someone dances right over it. There's a little crack in the corner of the screen, though who knows if that was there already. I'm far more interested in what's *on* the screen anyway: the ZigZag app. So that's what's been keeping him busy all night.

Look, I'm well aware that it's wrong to go snooping around in someone else's phone, but this holds the answers to almost all the questions that have been driving me crazy for days. I tap on Walker's ZigZag profile and hold my breath.

Except there's really nothing bad here. It's mostly photos of his tattoos. Lots of close-ups of the new scorpion piece. Apparently, the one on his leg is a python and the one on his back is a great white shark. He's fixated on predators, isn't he? Which is kind of disturbing, but I find myself feeling relieved, because this isn't what I expected to see. I expected to see evidence of other girls.

I guess I had no reason to worry after all.

Then a text message pops up on the screen. From Candice. His ex-girlfriend. And she's sending him a kissy-face emoji.

Um . . . what?

I tap it to open the whole conversation. Turns out they've been talking all night. Not about anything important. It's mostly memes and GIFs and emojis. Kissy-face emojis, to be exact. At one point, he says that he can't wait to see her again, and I'm finding it hard to believe that their encounter at that party last week was a total coincidence. I'm also finding it hard to believe she's really his ex.

Another text message appears. This time, it's not from Candice. It's from another girl named Jazmin. She's sent a selfie and captioned it, THINKIN OF U BB. Exactly how many girls has he been texting with tonight?

I open the whole conversation with Jazmin, then scroll back to see a message that makes me sick to my stomach: *when ur done with ur little math tutoring sesh, r u still comin over to my place?*

On stage, Taylor's strumming her guitar, the notes easily recognizable as the intro to "We Are Never Ever Getting Back Together." It's a song about second chances, how she keeps taking this guy back over and over again before finally realizing he'll never change. He's the same untrustworthy mess he's always been, and now she's tired and angry and totally done. I've never felt the gravity of those lyrics until this very moment.

As she breaks into the final chorus, Walker returns with this worried look on his face, which fades the instant he sees his phone in my hand. "There it is," he says.

I can barely hear him above the music and the screaming. He reaches out to take it back, but I don't hand it over. My fingers are wrapped around the phone case so tightly, I'm shocked it doesn't snap right in half.

Seeing Taylor Swift live in concert is most definitely a dream come true. But I'm beginning to feel like I never should've accepted these tickets. I'm not even sure what I'm doing here with Walker, or why he's interested in me. Or why I'm interested in him.

The energy inside the arena starts to shift. The screaming intensifies, the lights get brighter. Taylor takes center stage and thanks us for coming. Then a drumbeat kicks in and she starts to sing "Shake It Off." This must be the finale.

Everyone's going nuts, dancing and laughing and singing along, and once again, I feel as though Taylor understands me in a way no one else does. It's almost like she's singing this song right to me. *Players are always gonna play, Ashley. You've gotta just shake it off.*

But I don't want to shake it off. I want to scream.

"You're a jerk!"

He scrunches up his face, confused. I flip his phone around so he can see the screen, and he instantly gets pissy. "Why were you going through my text messages?"

"Screw you!" I chuck the phone at his chest and push my way into the aisle. The blinding flash of onstage pyrotechnics lights my way as I walk up the stairs. Confetti rains down, settling on my hair and my hoodie. I take one glance back at the stage, at Taylor striking her final pose, and I run toward the exit.

Walker doesn't catch up with me until I'm in the lobby. I don't stop when he calls my name, so he grabs my arm and spins me around. "Ashley, what the hell?"

"Don't touch me," I say, yanking my arm back.

"Why did you run out like that?"

"Because I don't know what I'm doing here."

"What are you talking about?"

"I mean, I don't know what I'm doing here with *you*. Or why you're here with me. What's your endgame here?"

"Endgame?"

"Yeah. Are you trying to turn this into some meaningless hookup? Or do you just want me to do your math homework for you?"

He looks as if I've slapped him across the face. "No, that's not it at all. I really like you. Like, I *like* you like you."

"Then why were you in there texting with all those other girls?"

"Why were you going through my phone?"

"I wasn't going through your phone. You dropped it and I picked it up so it didn't get trampled—you're welcome, by the way—and you happened to get a bunch of text messages while I was holding it in my hand. Kissy-faces and selfies. They didn't exactly seem platonic."

"Well, it's nice to feel wanted by *somebody*."

"What's that supposed to mean?"

"I can tell you're not into me, Ashley." I open my mouth to argue, but he cuts me off. "It's not like I blame you. You're smart and funny. Of course you don't like me. I'm an idiot for thinking you would. I'm an idiot, period."

"You're not an idiot."

He snickers. "Yeah, right. You spent forty-five minutes explaining an algebra problem to me the other day and I couldn't get it through my brain."

"Okay, well, you're bad at math."

"Yeah, and then I messed up your laptop because I was too stupid to know the difference between a legit video and a virus. I thought maybe taking you to this concert would change the way you felt about me, but I could tell as soon as we met up at the train station that nothing had changed. You pulled back as soon as I leaned in for a kiss." He shakes his head. "I don't know why you ran after me that morning when my dad was yelling at me. He's right. I'm a screwup."

"You're not a screwup."

He looks down at the ground, his lower lip quivering, like he's going to cry. I take his hand because I can't stand to see him looking so sad. He twines his fingers through mine and gives me a squeeze, and when his hazel eyes meet my gaze it occurs to me that maybe Walker isn't trouble at all. Maybe he's just troubled. There's a difference.

He smiles a watery smile, like he's still sort of drunk, and plucks a piece of stray confetti from my hair. He shows it to me, then lets it flutter to the ground. It reminds me of that moment in Ms. Henley's class, back when I thought Walker Beech was the most perfect guy on the planet. Turns out, I couldn't have been more wrong.

And we are never, ever getting back together.

Now that the adrenaline rush of the concert has worn off, I can't wait to get into bed and go to sleep. We head outside, where the night air is crisp. I put up my hood and Walker wraps his arm around my shoulders. "Are you cold?"

"No, I'm fine." I don't want him to hug me. I just want to get on the train and go home. But before I can wriggle out of his embrace, he steers me away from the subway entrance and turns toward Sixth Avenue. "Where are we going?"

He's futzing around with his phone again. I want to grab it from his hands and toss it into traffic. "There's a Lyft waiting for us on the corner of Pacific," he says.

"A Lyft?"

"My treat." He's acting like it's totally normal to be taking a forty-dollar car service home from a concert. Does he do this all the time? How does he even have a Lyft account? You're not supposed to have one until you're eighteen.

Then again, this is Walker Beech we're talking about. He snags Taylor Swift tickets on a moment's notice and buys beer like it's no big deal. He hangs out in tattoo shops and gets Ms. Henley to smile. Regular rules don't apply to him.

But a ride home is a ride home, and I'm certainly not too keen on getting on the subway by myself right now. There's a white Toyota sedan idling halfway down the block, lights blazing, purple Lyft sign glowing on the dash. Walker opens the back door and lets me in first. The driver nods his head, a silent hello, then presses the button on his app to start the trip.

It's funny. The me of two weeks ago would've died for a chance to be in the backseat of a car with Walker Beech. Now I can't wait for this ride to be over. I should tell the driver to drop me off first.

My phone buzzes with a text from Mom: *Let me know how the show was!* I text back: *Amazing! Omw home now.*

We turn a corner and the streets suddenly look very familiar. We're nowhere near home, that I know for sure, but I feel like I've been here recently. There are trees and construction cones and a building that kinda looks like a courthouse.

Wait. I have been here recently. With Jason. The night we walked across the Brooklyn Bridge.

I wonder what he's doing tonight. If he's hanging out with

Rachel. Would he ever surprise her with a romantic walk across the Brooklyn Bridge? The idea of it makes me feel queasy.

We hang a left and start speeding up, and it takes me a minute to realize we're on an entrance ramp to some sort of highway. There's an elevated pedestrian promenade beside us, with people walking and biking and taking pictures. Soon One World Trade comes into view. Then I realize we're not going home at all.

We're driving over the Brooklyn Bridge.

Chapter Twenty-One

"Are we going into the city?" I try not to sound panicky, and fail.

"Yeah. Don't you wanna keep hanging out?"

Considering we just had an epic fight in the middle of the Barclays Center? "No, I wanna go home."

"But it's only eleven. It's still early."

"It's an hour past my regular curfew."

He furrows his brow. "You have a curfew?"

"I told you that the other day!"

"Yeah, but I thought you were making that up. You mean you really *did* go home after you got your tattoo?"

"Yes! My mom is super strict. She made an exception for the concert tonight, but . . ."

Oh no. Mom.

I already told her I was on my way home. If she sees I'm headed in the opposite direction, she'll kill me. In an instant, I whip out my phone and turn off the location. I'd rather make up some story about a faulty GPS than explain why I took a detour through Manhattan.

"Come on." He slides closer and I slide farther away so I'm practically hanging my head out the window. "Let's go to Jimmy's for one drink," he says.

"Who's Jimmy?"

"It's this club in the Village. They're pretty easy about the whole ID thing."

In the rearview mirror, the driver's eyes flash to mine. I look away and mutter, "I don't have a fake ID."

Walker laughs. A full-on cackle, like I'm the most ridiculous person in the world. "What? That's crazy."

"Well, I don't. Let's go home."

"We're in the middle of the Brooklyn Bridge. We can't exactly pull over."

He's right. There aren't any service lanes here, and there's nowhere to make a U-turn. We're headed into Manhattan tonight, whether I like it or not.

I've always considered myself to be pretty sharp. The kind of street-smart New Yorker who can see trouble coming from a mile away. But that day in Ms. Henley's class, when Jason set off the confetti cannon, I never once suspected Walker Beech would be the real troublemaker.

The New York City skyline grows closer and closer, and finally, after what feels like an eternity, we're pulling off an exit ramp and taking a long circular road that dumps us into lower Manhattan.

"You know, it'll be fine," Walker says. "They'll probably let you in without an ID."

"No." My voice is stronger and stonier than it's ever sounded. "I want to go home."

At the first red light, I ask the driver to end the ride. He makes eye contact with me in the rearview mirror as he pulls to the curb. "Everything okay, Miss?" he asks, and I know what he really means. *Do you need help? Are you in trouble?*

"Thanks, but I'm okay." I'm not okay, but I need to get out of this car, immediately. Walker gets out behind me, the car drives off, and then we're alone. Or as alone as one can ever be on a Manhattan street, even on a Wednesday after eleven p.m.

I have absolutely no idea where we are. There's a park to our right and a Starbucks across the street, but no obvious landmarks. Nothing that says YOU ARE HERE. I probably should've told the driver to turn around and drive us back to Brooklyn, but it's too late for that now.

"Can you get another Lyft to bring us home?" I ask.

"You sure you don't wanna hang out? We don't have to go to Jimmy's. We can hang out here."

He nods toward the entrance to the park. I peek through the wrought-iron fence. There aren't many people in there, and the ones who are there don't seem particularly friendly. One guy's muttering under his breath while shredding newspapers into tiny pieces. Why does he want to hang out in a dark park in the middle of a Wednesday night?

Suddenly, I feel his hand on my waist and his breath in my ear.

Oh, that's why.

I sidestep his touch and whirl around. "What are you doing?"

"Let's hang out a little longer."

"I told you, I have a curfew. And besides that, I'm not interested in whatever you want to do right now."

"You're sending a lot of mixed messages," he says. "You know, if you weren't interested, you shouldn't have taken those concert tickets in the first place."

"You told me they were to make up for the fact that you

messed up my laptop! And did you honestly think I was going to make out with you in the middle of the night in this shady public park? What is wrong with you?"

He sucks his teeth, and it occurs to me that Walker could be both troubled and trouble at the exact same time.

"I'm going to walk away," I say. "And I don't want you to follow me."

Before I can change my mind, I spin on my heel and hurry off through the park. Walker's calling my name, but I keep moving forward. Past the guy shredding newspapers and muttering to himself, past another person asleep on a bench. The tree trunks look menacing, like someone could pop out from behind one at any moment. Perhaps it wasn't the smartest idea to wander into a park by myself at night.

There's no turning back, though, so I pick up the pace, from a brisk walk to a jog to a full-on sprint. By the time I emerge on the other side of the park, I'm panting and wheezing. Exhausted, but in the clear.

I pause on the sidewalk to catch my breath. It's slightly more crowded out here, but not very. I don't want to be with Walker right now, but I also don't want to be alone.

There's yet another Starbucks across the street, but all the lights are off inside. One block up, there's a Duane Reade that appears to be open, so I take off running again. When the automatic doors slide open to welcome me in, I've never felt more grateful for the existence of twenty-four-hour drugstores.

The man behind the cash register looks up from his phone long enough to side-eye me, then goes back to whatever he was doing. Out of habit, I wander off toward the makeup aisle. Somewhere between the eyeliner and the lip gloss, I stop and realize I have no clue what to do next.

In the movies, when kids find themselves in trouble in the middle of the night, they usually call their moms or dads to come pick them up. Those kids usually live in the suburbs and their parents have cars. My mom doesn't have a car.

But my dad does.

I know he's unreliable and emotionally unavailable, and I know he will never, ever change. But I need his help now, and that tiny little girl living inside my brain is whispering her usual line: "Maybe he'll show up this time!" So I dial his number and listen as it rings and rings and rings.

I'm about to hang up when he finally answers. "Ashley? What are you doing calling so late?"

His speech is kind of slurred and I can hear Stefanie whining in the background, "Richie, who is that? What's going on?" There's a low rumble in the background, like he's in a crowd of people. And are those steel drums playing?

Oh, right. He's at a Club Med in the Bahamas, soaking up the sun with Stefanie and Axel and Milo, enjoying his family-friendly spring break without me.

"Ashley? Are you okay?"

My dad never asks if I'm okay. Granted, I never call him in the middle of the night. Still, Dad and I never talk about feelings. But I'm having a whole lot of feelings right now, and I'm finding it really hard to keep them inside.

"Why didn't you invite me to the Bahamas?"

There's a pause, and all I hear are steel drums. Then, as if he couldn't understand the question, he says, "What?"

"Why didn't you invite me along on your family vacation?" I hate that my voice is warbling, but I can't help it. "I'm part of your family."

"Of course you're part of my family. You're my only daughter." The background is getting quiet now, like he moved to an emptier space. I picture him standing beside a palm tree on a sandy beach, a salty sea breeze rustling his hair. I've never been to the Caribbean before.

"I know Stefanie doesn't like me."

"She likes you, of course she—"

"Dad, stop. There's no point in lying. And I mean, fine, she doesn't like me, but . . ." I breathe deeply, swallowing a sob. "It would've been nice to be included, that's all. To feel like you actually care about me."

"I care about you, sweetie."

"It doesn't feel that way. You blow me off every other weekend. And when you do show up, you don't listen to anything I say. You never tell me I'm doing a good job or ask me how I'm feeling. You don't have to be interested in my life, Dad, but you can at least pretend. For me."

He doesn't say anything. I can hear him breathing, or maybe that's just a gust of wind coming from the ocean. Finally, he speaks my name, but I end the call before he can say anything else. Because I realize I don't care what he has to say for himself. I've unloaded my emotions. They're his burden to bear now.

But I'm not feeling any better, because I'm still stuck here in a Duane Reade with no way to get home.

I don't have the money for a yellow cab. I suppose I could take the subway, but it's midnight, and the train isn't running very often, if it's even running at all. Plus, I was scared out of my mind just walking through a park. I can't imagine navigating the labyrinth of the New York City subway system right now.

Maybe I can stay here all night. It's safe back here in the makeup aisle. I'm not bothering anybody.

As I contemplate constructing a bed out of cosmetic sponges and cotton balls, my phone dings three times in a row.

> Where are you? Your phone location is off.
> Your father just called. He said you were crying.
> Are you okay????

The phone rings in my hand. Her voice is panicked. "Where are you? What happened?"

"I'm in Manhattan, at some Duane Reade, but I don't know where."

"How did you end up there? Where's Christine?"

"Christine's not here. I didn't go to the concert with Christine tonight, I went with Walker. And we got in a fight and now . . . I'm here."

"Did he hurt you?"

"No, I'm fine, I promise."

There's silence on the other end of the phone. Then I hear her take a deep breath and let it out. "Turn on your phone location. I'm coming to get you."

"But how? I can just take the train, or—"

"The hell you're taking the train! Stay right where you are. Do not move. I'll be there as soon as I can."

She hangs up. I turn on my location and wait for my mom in the makeup aisle. I'm assuming she's taking a Lyft, which is going to cost a small fortune. I'm sure she'll make me pay her back. Even if she doesn't make me, I will.

Twenty minutes later, I get another text. *I'm outside. Come quick.*

The cashier side-eyes me as I rush out the door. There's only one car at the curb, and it doesn't have a purple Lyft sign glowing on the dash. It's a gray Buick with a scratched-up bumper. I know this car. It's Mrs. Eisler's.

Mom's behind the wheel, so I get in the passenger seat. Her eyes are tired, and her lips are a fine line.

"I'm really sorry, Mom."

She doesn't say anything. Somehow, the silent treatment is worse than being scolded. I can't stand the quiet, so I start explaining what happened, but she cuts me off immediately.

"I can't talk about this right now, Ashley. I need to focus on the road. I worked all day and I'm tired. We don't all get the luxury of a spring break."

This shuts me up.

"We'll discuss this tomorrow," she says, "after I get home from work. You are not to leave the house until I get home. Do you understand?"

"Yes."

We don't speak for the rest of the ride. When we get back to our building, she parks Mrs. Eisler's car in her assigned spot underground, then goes straight to her bedroom and shuts the door. I do the same.

My clothes suddenly feel dirty. I need to get out of them as soon as possible. As I unzip my hoodie, I glance in the mirror that hangs over my dresser and notice something's missing.

My paper airplane necklace.

I touch the spot near my throat where it should be dangling. I've lost it somewhere. Maybe at the Barclays Center, maybe in the park. Who knows? All I know is it's gone, forever.

And I can't help but think that I got what I deserve.

Chapter Twenty-Two

The next day, I sleep until noon. When I wake up, there aren't any messages waiting for me on my phone. Mom hasn't called or texted, though I'm sure she's checked my location a thousand times. Not that I blame her. I've probably lost her trust forever.

I don't feel like getting up or taking a shower or changing out of my pajamas or even brushing my teeth. But I can't just lie here staring at the ceiling all day. The hackathon starts tomorrow morning. I've only got a few hours left to prepare.

So even though I feel trapped in a self-made swamp of despair, I manage to fire up my laptop. Then, from the safety and comfort of my bed, I spend the whole afternoon working through coding exercises and ZigZag documentation. For a little while, I actually feel okay. Studying takes my mind off the train wreck my life has become, and after a few hours of losing myself in hackathon prep, I think maybe everything's gonna be all right.

Until I hear the scrape of Mom's key in the front door locks. The door slams, her keys and purse land on the kitchen table, her footsteps echo down the hallway. I'm holding my breath when she opens my bedroom door. She doesn't knock, and she doesn't look happy.

"We need to talk," she says, not quite meeting my eyes. "Let's sit in the kitchen."

I follow her silently down the hallway and we sit in our usual spots at the table. She's frowning, but she doesn't seem angry. If anything, she seems sad. Like she's disappointed in me. I wish she were angry instead.

"Would you like to tell me why you lied to me about where you were going last night?"

"I didn't lie. I went to the concert. It's just afterward, Walker took me into the city. I told him I had to go home, but—"

"You told me you were going to the concert with Christine. Was she there last night?"

"No."

"So you *did* lie."

"If I told you I was going with Walker, you wouldn't have let me go."

"You're right, I wouldn't have, and considering how your night ended up, that would've been the right decision." She squeezes her hands into fists, then releases them. "Why did you call your father? Why didn't you call me first?"

"Because he has a car. I thought he could pick me up. I forgot he was going to the Bahamas."

"So how did you wind up in a Duane Reade in the Financial District?"

"Walker got a Lyft. I thought he was taking me home, but before I knew it, we were driving over the Brooklyn Bridge. We got in this huge fight in the car, and I hopped out at a red light. Then he followed me, so I ran away, but it was dark and

I was scared so I went to the drugstore because it was open and I didn't know what else to do."

She shakes her head. "What would possess you to get into a car with this boy? Just the other day, you told me he was a liar."

"Well, I thought he changed. He apologized and seemed sincere about it. But obviously I was wrong. I feel like an idiot for ever getting involved with him in the first place."

My voice falters and Mom's eyes soften around the edges. "Ashley, what's going on with you lately? Ever since you got rejected from that internship, you haven't been acting like yourself. You're lying, you're hanging out with bad people. Is this what you want out of life?"

Funny, I always thought I knew what I wanted out of life. My vision board made my goals crystal clear. A degree from Stanford or Berkeley, followed by a job in Silicon Valley, where I'd live in a house with a big backyard. As soon as I ripped up my vision board, things started going sideways. That's probably not a coincidence.

"I don't know anymore," I say, burying my face in my hands.

Mom strokes the back of my head, and in a gentle voice, says, "I know the thing with ZigZag was a disappointment, but you have to move on from it. You have to have new dreams to work toward. Because if you don't have your own, you'll get tangled up in someone else's."

The tears flow freely now. Mom's hands feel warm and comforting as she runs her fingers through my hair. Mom's strict and it drives me crazy, but at least I know she cares.

Suddenly, she stops stroking my hair, and in a significantly less gentle voice, she says, "This had better be temporary."

Oh no. My tattoo.

I'd been so caught up in my anguish, I'd forgotten all about keeping it hidden. Now my hair's fallen off to the side and the back of my neck is in full view and oh god Mom's nostrils are flaring. This is not gonna be good.

"When did you get this?"

"Last week."

"When you went out with Walker?"

"Yes, but—"

She slams her hands on the kitchen table and I nearly fall out of my chair. "Okay! I see this is far worse than I could've imagined."

"It's just a tattoo, Mom, it's not—"

"*Just* a tattoo? A tattoo is a permanent mark on your skin, Ashley. It is never going away. Unless you want to get a very expensive, very painful laser procedure, which, by the way, I'm not paying for."

"But I don't want to get it removed." I really don't. Despite the fact that it will forever remind me of my first ill-fated date with Walker, it's still meaningful, personal, and unique. It's a symbol that represents who I am and what's important to me.

Mom's not buying it, though.

"You're grounded for the rest of spring break," she says. "The only places you're allowed to go are ShopRite and the library. Socializing's off-limits. And if you turn your phone location off *once*, I'm taking it away."

"Fine." I'm not thrilled, but I'm not exactly devastated, either. It's not like I had much socializing planned for the next few days. Except . . . "I can still go to the hackathon, right?"

"Absolutely not."

She can't be serious. "But it's not a social event."

"Of course it is. It's a sleepover in a room full of teenagers who all happen to be coding at the same time."

No. No, no, no. "Mom, the prize. The ZigZag internship. I've been preparing for this all week. It's my second chance at getting into their summer program."

Her laugh is stilted and bitter. "You can't travel to the other side of the borough without lying to me through your teeth. You think I'll let you travel to the other side of the *country*? No way."

If only she'd confiscate my phone. Reduce my curfew time. Make me clean the bathroom sink and scrub the toilet bowl. Anything but this.

"That's not fair."

"It is entirely fair. Trust is something you earn, Ashley. And there's nothing worse than a liar."

She stands up, a sign that we're done here. The ruling is final and cannot be appealed. I storm off to my room, tears already streaking down my cheeks. I want to hate Mom, but more than anything I hate myself. Everything she said was right. I can't argue with the truth.

I've thrown away a second chance at my dream come true.

My laptop's still open on my bed. I slap it closed, since there's no point in doing any work now. There's a sticker on the top: PROPERTY OF MR. PODONSKY'S WORKSHOP. What will Mr. P think when he sees I'm not at the hackathon tomorrow?

The sight of it is painful, so I close my eyes, pull on my headphones, and load up a playlist I created called "Every Taylor Swift Song Ever Recorded." Then I press Play and lie faceup on my bedroom floor. I close my eyes and turn the volume up as high as I can stand, until the music penetrates every crevice and ridge of my brain.

Once again, I feel as though Taylor understands me in a way no one else does. When "I Knew You Were Trouble" comes on, and she starts singing about mistakes and blame and shame, I've never felt more seen in my entire life. Deep down, I knew Walker was trouble, but I ignored my better judgment. I made bad decision after bad decision—lying to Mom, loaning Walker my laptop, getting in a car with him, lying to Mom *again*. Every bad thing that happened was really all my fault.

The song fades out and transitions into the opening drumbeat of "Lover." My heart aches, remembering the last time I listened to this song in this room. My hoodie flashing, Jason staring at me like I was the most beautiful person on earth. He's probably with Rachel right now, making *her* feel like the most beautiful person on earth.

I was a fool not to tell him how I felt when I had the chance. Another opportunity squandered.

She's singing the bridge now, all about hearts that are borrowed and blue, and my eyes are swollen with tears. I squeeze them shut even tighter, in a vain attempt to stop myself from crying. There's no holding it back, though.

When I'm all cried out, I open my eyes. My vision's blurry, but through the teary haze, I clearly see the person standing in my doorway.

Jason.

I'm not even surprised he's here. It's like I summoned him with the power of my yearning.

"Hi." My voice is froggy. I sit up and take off my headphones.

"Hi." He takes a step forward, then another one. "How are you?"

I don't know how to answer him. He must know what happened. Mom borrowed his mom's car in the middle of the night. I'm sure he asked questions. What am I supposed to say?

He comes toward me, slowly, with his hand outstretched. Like he's reaching out for me. I almost take hold of him, but then I see something dangling off the tip of his index finger. Something small and shiny and silver.

"My necklace." The paper airplane that I thought was gone forever. It's in the palm of Jason's hand. I jump to my feet, then grab the necklace and hold it tightly to my chest. "Thank you! Where did you find it?"

"On the floor of my mom's car." He scratches the back of his neck. "I guess it fell off last night."

"Yeah." I swallow hard. "Last night sucked."

"I heard you went to a Taylor Swift concert, though. Couldn't have been all bad."

"The concert was good. Nothing else was."

He looks down at his feet, then back at me, fixing me with his chocolate-brown eyes. I want nothing more than to tell him I love him.

"You were right about Walker," I say, the words coming out in a rush. "He's a jerk. I don't like him like that, either. I don't even know why I—"

"It's okay." Jason puts his hand up, a gentle signal to stop talking. "You don't have to explain."

I know I don't *have* to explain. I *want* to explain. But maybe Jason doesn't want to hear it. Maybe he just doesn't care.

Because he doesn't love me the way I love him.

Suddenly, I feel self-conscious. It's six o'clock at night and I haven't brushed my teeth today and I'm still wearing my rumpled, smelly pajamas.

He clears his throat. "I've gotta get home. Mom's putting dinner on the table. I just wanted to give that back to you. I know you love that necklace."

Of course he knows. He knows everything about me. Except how I really feel about him.

I want to tell him right now, but he turns around and walks down the hallway before I can drum up the courage. He stalks to the front door, passing the kitchen, where Mom's putting something in the microwave. "Bye, Jason," she says.

"Bye." With his hand on the doorknob, he turns to me and says, "I'll see you tomorrow. The hackathon starts at noon. Wanna take the train in together?"

My mouth is moving but there aren't any words coming out. It's like my vocal cords are paralyzed, unwilling to accept the truth.

Mom plops two plates on the table and calls out, "She's not going tomorrow."

He furrows his brow, looking from me to Mom and back again. "What? Why?"

"Because of what she pulled last night." She's practically slamming the forks and knives onto our place settings. "Ashley's grounded for the rest of spring break."

"You can't do that," he says, stepping back into the kitchen. If only I had half his courage.

Mom does not look amused. "I certainly can."

"But it's not just about Ashley. We've got a team all set up and ready to go. Without her, there's no way we can win." My heart does a little pitter-patter when he glances my way. "We need her."

My mom is always quick with the comebacks, so the fact that she's pausing right now gives me hope. Maybe Jason will change her mind.

"There are three other people counting on her to be there," he says.

"Two," I say quickly, not wanting Mom to think I was lying about that, too. "Two other people. You and Christine."

"No, three. Rachel's coming, too."

"What?"

"Don't worry, I talked to Christine about it. She's on board."

He smiles, like I'm supposed to be happy about this. But I'm not happy, not at all. Rachel Gibbons is competing on *my* hackathon team while I have to stay home.

I turn to Mom and plead. "Please, let me go. You heard him, the team is counting on me."

She crosses her arms against her chest and heaves out an exasperated breath. "All right. You can go. But you're going straight there and straight home, and you better check in with me regularly." Her eyes snap to Jason. "And I'm counting on you, too. If you mess this up, I'm going to your parents. Don't think I won't."

"Of course." He nods, then says to me, "Let's leave at eleven, okay? I wanna get there early, get our stuff all set up."

"Sure thing." As he steps out into the hall, I whisper, "Thank you. For everything."

He looks at me, and I almost say it. I almost tell him I love him.

But then I don't, because now's not the time to be feeling my feelings. Now's the time to be focusing on my goals. And right now, my most important goal is to win first prize in this hackathon. Even if it means joining forces with my true love's girlfriend.

Chapter Twenty-Three

The New York City High School Spring Break Hackathon (sponsored by ZigZag Technologies Inc.) is being held at the MakerSpace of NYU's engineering school in downtown Brooklyn. From home, it's a straight shot on the F train, only about a half hour away.

On Friday morning, Jason and I leave at eleven o'clock on the dot, laptops and sleeping bags in tow. We don't talk much on the ride in. I'm trying to conserve all my energy for the competition.

Also, Jason's preoccupied with his phone. Probably texting Rachel or something.

But I cannot let this upset me. Getting caught up in my feelings about Rachel and Jason will throw me off my game and jeopardize my chances of winning the internship. Now's the time to focus! I close my eyes and quiz myself on some of the more prominent features of ZigZag. I've practiced a lot, and I'm feeling pretty confident right about now.

I'm not sure how Jason's feeling, though. I haven't asked him.

When the train pulls into the MetroTech center, we climb

the stairs and exit onto Jay Street. There's a huge, red, geometric sculpture in the center of a pedestrian plaza, alongside a sign that reads HACKATHON THIS WAY, pointing toward the building to our left. A bunch of kids our age are filing through a revolving glass door. Mostly boys, but some girls too. They have laptop bags and sleeping bags and backpacks. All of them, my competition.

We follow the crowd inside to the lobby, where there's a long line for the registration desk. I don't see Christine anywhere. Or Rachel. Or anyone else from our school, for that matter. This place is so packed. There are way more people here than I thought there'd be.

Am I in over my head? Sure, I'm smart and I get good grades and everything, but my whole academic life exists within the confines of Murrow's hallways. Maybe my status as a high achiever is a big fish–little pond type of situation. Once you take me out of Murrow, I'm just your average Jane.

And that's a problem, because students from some of the best schools in the city are here. One kid's wearing a Stuyvesant hoodie, and those guys in the button-down shirts *must* be from some private school somewhere in Manhattan. I'll bet they come from rich families. Who knows if they bribed someone to be here?

Whatever. I'll beat them all.

Jason nudges me with his elbow. "Imagine setting off a stink bomb in here."

Oh no. "If you pull a prank during this hackathon, I will never speak to you again."

"I'm not going to, don't worry. But if I were, these *would* be the perfect conditions." He gets this wistful look on his face, imagining the possibilities.

After what seems like an eternity, we finally get to the front of the line. A woman signs us in and hands us swag bags, then sends us off to a large room down the hall. It's cavernous and crowded, with at least a dozen rows of long, rectangular tables. Each table must have fifty chairs around it, maybe more. The echo of chatter and laughter makes it hard to think straight.

I scan the sea of faces and find Christine sitting at a table halfway across the conference hall. She's chatting with a guy I've never seen before. They're both laughing, and she just put her hand on his arm. If I didn't know any better, I'd think she was flirting. That's not something Christine does. Like, ever.

"There she is," I say, but Jason's got his nose buried in his phone.

"Who?" He looks over at Christine, then says, "Oh. I'll come meet you guys in a sec. I'm gonna go wait for Rachel by the entrance. Make sure she finds us okay."

"Okay."

I cannot let this upset me.

Christine's staked out a spot at the end of a table, her laptop already booted. She's still giggling when I sit down across from her. "Hey," I say.

She jolts, like I've scared her. "Oh, hey. Um, Ashley, this is Ahmad. We met at a science camp a couple of years ago. Ahmad, this is my best friend, Ashley."

"Nice to meet you, Ashley." Ahmad smiles at me, and I notice how bright and straight his teeth are. His eyes are sort of greenish, too, and his eyebrows are dark and thick but extraordinarily well maintained. He's really cute.

"Nice to meet you too."

"I should be getting back to my team." He points vaguely

behind him, then gazes at Christine in a way that makes my chest ache. "I'll see you around?"

"Yeah. See you around." She watches as he walks away, still staring at the space he left behind long before he's disappeared into the crowd. I clear my throat to get her attention, and when she sees the way I'm raising my eyebrows, she says, "What?"

"Christine Kong, are you *flirting* with a high school boy?"

"No! We're just friends." She turns her attention to her laptop and starts tapping at the keyboard, then quickly adds, "He's very mature, by the way."

"I'm sure he is."

"Isn't this turnout insane?" she says, glancing around the room. "I did *not* expect this many people to show up."

"Me neither. Do you think we have a chance of winning?"

"Oh, for sure. I'll bet half these people don't even know how to code. They probably signed up at the last minute just for the ZigZag swag."

I can't help myself. "Like Rachel Gibbons?"

"Yeah, but she's not just an average ZigZag user, you know? She's got, like, thousands of followers. I'm sure she'll have a lot of really good ideas to help us out." She narrows her eyes at me. "Why are you acting all mad about it, anyway? Jason told me you were fine with her being on the team. He said he just wanted to run it by me."

"Who's mad? I'm not mad." I am totally mad.

But I cannot let this upset me.

Instead, I turn my attention to the panel of judges assembling behind the dais at the front of the room. There are five people, only one of them a woman. I don't recognize any of them. I kind of hoped the CEO of ZigZag would show up, but I'm sure a billionaire like him has better things to do with his time.

"Do you know who's who?" I ask Christine, nodding toward the judges.

She looks over and shrugs. "No clue."

I've got an urge to go over and introduce myself, to find out which one's on the software engineering team. Would that make the judges think I'm proactive and motivated, or would I just seem like a suck-up? I can't tell, so I do nothing.

As I'm setting up my work space—laptop, headphones, notepad, and sharpened pencils—Jason returns. Rachel's beaming at his side, wearing a really cute skirtall. Now I know where Jason got it for his blow-up-doll prank.

"Hi!" She slides in next to me, all smiles and sunny disposition. Her hair is in a messy half topknot that looks so cool on her and that I could never pull off. "This is *so* exciting. I can't believe how many people are here."

Jason sits across from Rachel, next to Christine. "We've got a lot of competition."

"Don't worry," Christine says, glancing my way. "We'll crush them all."

Popping open his swag bag, Jason says, "Wonder what kinda loot we scored." The rest of us open our bags, too. Rachel is clearly in heaven. With each new find, she lets loose with a squee.

Vinyl stickers printed with the ZigZag logo? "Eee!"

Stuffed sloth wearing a ZigZag T-shirt? "Eee!"

I try to block her out by reviewing the brochure that details the hackathon's schedule of events. The opening ceremony will be starting any minute, followed by two hours of networking and brainstorming, then some lectures and workshops for people who need help or want to learn some new tech. At six o'clock, we break for dinner. After that, it's nonstop coding.

"We'll have time to assemble our prototypes and practice our presentations in the morning," I say. "Then, final demos start at noon."

"When do the judges announce the winners?" Christine asks.

"At two o'clock." I slap the brochure closed. "A little over twenty-four hours from now. We have to use every second wisely. Everybody got their laptops booted?"

"Ready to go," Christine says.

"Getting there," Jason says.

I turn to Rachel for an answer, but she's no longer sitting next to me. For a moment, I'm relieved. Maybe all she came for was the swag bag, and once she got her sticker and stuffed sloth, she took off.

Then I see her. Over at the dais, schmoozing with two of the judges. She says something undoubtedly witty and charming and they laugh.

Suck-up.

As she heads back to our table, a woman steps up to the podium beside the dais. Her voice comes over the microphone, clear but soft. "Hello? Hello there. If I could have your attention, please?"

It takes a minute, and a bunch of people yelling out "Be quiet!" but a hush eventually falls over the room. The woman continues, "Hello, my name is Tara Osman, I'm a professor of computer science here at NYU, and also the chief organizer of the New York City High School Spring Break Hackathon."

Cheers erupt around the room. When they die down, she continues. "I'd like to welcome you all here, and thank you for being a part of this inspiring and inclusive event. We have participants from all five boroughs, and I'm really looking forward to getting to know each and every one of you over the course of the next twenty-four hours.

"I'd also like to thank ZigZag"—more cheers, more waiting for them to die down—"for so generously swooping in at the last minute to provide us with a panel of four judges and some much-needed sponsorship dollars. I hope everyone likes their swag bags." She says the word *swag* like it's a dirty word she's not sure she should be broadcasting to a room full of teenagers. Rachel waves her sloth in the air and whoops.

Suck-up.

Professor Osman then reviews some of the rules we already know. Teams can consist of two to four people, and if you don't currently have a team, you can take advantage of the networking and brainstorming period to find one. All work must be new and original, meaning you can't reuse any code, graphics, or written material you or anyone else has created before you walked in this room. You can't work remotely with other users, either, which means phone calls and chat programs are banned. ZigZag will be providing a problem to solve, and all prototypes must be submitted by 11:59 tomorrow morning to be considered for the competition.

"Food will be served in the conference room down the hall, and if you need to take a nap, there's a designated quiet space on the second floor.

"And now," she says, "without further ado, I'd like to introduce the head of product development for ZigZag, Mr. James Lee."

The crowd starts cheering again. A man who doesn't look all that much older than us approaches the podium. He waves and adjusts the microphone up to his height.

"Hello, everybody! Welcome! Thanks for being a part of

this exciting event!" His voice is so full of enthusiasm, I can almost hear the exclamation point at the end of every sentence. "Show of hands: How many of you are ZigZag users?"

Every hand shoots in the air.

"Awesome! That's what we like to see! At ZigZag, we know how important it is for you to stay connected, express yourself, and share your brilliant ideas with the world! That's why we're here today! To help you help us improve your ZigZag experience!

"ZigZag is always adding new features and fixing old problems so we can continue to maintain our status as the number one social media app in the United States. As the head of product development, I'm responsible for overseeing all those changes and enhancements. So I'm constantly asking myself: how can ZigZag better meet the needs of our users?

"That's where this hackathon comes in! Your goal is to come up with a way to use ZigZag to solve a common problem affecting you and your peers. Think about what you've been going through lately. Your struggles, your frustrations. What's been bugging you? What roadblocks are in your way? Then, once you've identified your problem, design a technical solution using ZigZag's API that will help to solve it!"

An excited buzz crackles around the room. Some people are squinting like they're confused. Others are already tapping away at their laptop keyboards, letting their ideas flow freely. I feel a surge of confidence. We've got this. Christine, Jason, and I have been studying the API all week.

Evidently, though, Rachel hasn't. "What's an API?" she asks, stroking the stuffed sloth on its fuzzy little head.

"An application programming interface." I tap at the touch pad on my laptop to open a blank document. "I was thinking we could generate an idea by doing a massive brain dump. Like you guys start talking and I'll take notes, then we can sort through it all when we're done."

"Good idea," Christine says.

I glance over at Jason to see what he thinks, but I'm pretty sure he didn't hear me. He's too distracted by Rachel, who's now inching her sloth across the table, as if it's crawling toward him very, very slowly. Then she tilts it forward, so its smiling face touches the back of his hand. She makes a kissing sound, and I think I'm gonna hurl.

Okay. It's only twenty-four hours. I can deal with this for twenty-four hours, if it means scoring an internship at ZigZag.

Except it's only just occurred to me that if this team wins the internship, I'll be forced to endure an entire summer with Rachel and Jason, watching their annoying PDA all over Silicon Valley. This is a nightmare.

Still. I cannot let it upset me.

I have a goal to achieve. With my fingers positioned over my keyboard, I say, "Let's start brainstorming."

Chapter Twenty-Four

We've been brainstorming for forty-five minutes. Our list of problems is long—overcrowded buses, boring classes, ridiculously early curfews—but we're having trouble choosing which one to solve. The seconds are zooming by, and we've got to decide soon or we'll never finish in time.

I wish there was an app to make this decision for us.

Oh. That's it!

"I have a really great idea," I say.

"What is it?" Christine asks.

"Well, we all have trouble making decisions, right? When we're overwhelmed with choices, sometimes it can be hard to pick the best one. Look at us right now. We've got so much at stake that we're afraid of making the wrong choice, so we're not making any choice at all. Wouldn't it be great to get an outside opinion from someone who doesn't have skin in the game?"

"We're not allowed to get an outside opinion," Jason says. "Remember? They said we can't work remotely with other people."

"I don't mean for us to get an outside opinion *now*. That

was just an example. But what about in other areas of our lives? We're overwhelmed with choices all the time, like deciding which extracurriculars to take or which college to go to. We could create an app to crowdsource the answers by hooking into ZigZag and asking your followers to help you out. They can list pros and cons, offer suggestions, and encourage you when you're feeling insecure."

"Ooh, I like that," Christine says. "It could work not only for big-picture decision-making but also smaller, everyday choices, too."

"Exactly. And it can help you to avoid making bad, impulsive decisions."

"Like getting a tattoo?" The snark in Jason's voice is unmistakable.

"Yeah," I say. "Or setting off a confetti cannon in the middle of class."

He scowls, and Rachel interjects, "I kind of like that idea, but I think we should make the decision more focused."

"What does that mean?"

"Well, ZigZag users are really into fashion. They're always posting outfit-of-the-day selfies and sharing styling tips and stuff. What if we made an app that just helped people decide what to wear to school that day?"

"Well, in theory, this decision-making app could do that, but it would also include other stuff, too. Why would we limit ourselves?"

She gives me an incredulous look, like the answer should be obvious. "So ZigZag can monetize the app. We'll make it into something so much more than just a decision-maker. It'll be a whole shopping experience. We can include links to buy the clothes, and ZigZag will get a cut of whatever sales they make."

I stare at her, completely bewildered. We're not here to write a shopping app. We're here to solve a real-world problem. I'm about to dismiss the idea out of hand, when Christine says, "I like it."

Rachel smiles triumphantly as I turn to Christine and say, "Really?"

"Yeah. Remember, advertising is how ZigZag makes most of their money, and this app would basically be one big clothing advertisement. The judges will eat it up."

"And," Rachel adds, "it addresses a struggle we each face in our everyday lives."

It's hard to keep from rolling my eyes. "I wouldn't call deciding what to wear a struggle."

Rachel looks me up and down, taking in my baseball tee, my mussed-up ponytail, my decidedly uncool glasses. Her expression speaks for itself. Maybe I *could* use some help crowdsourcing my outfits.

Still, "I'm not sure this really addresses the hackathon challenge."

"Of course it does," Jason says. "And I think it's fair to say that Rachel knows how people use ZigZag more than anyone else on our team."

The fact that he's defending her makes me feel two inches tall. I shrink further when Rachel asks, "How many followers do *you* have, Ashley?"

"Um . . ." I don't know. Something like . . . "Fifty, maybe?" Though now that I think about it, it's probably not that many.

"Right." She nods, smiling. "I have 24,659. So."

I guess that makes her the ZigZag expert.

It seems like everyone else is Team Rachel, and I'm not about to be the troublemaker. So I say, "Fine. Let's do that.

We should probably start gathering requirements next. Detailing all the things we want the app to do. Then we can convert those to individual tasks and add them to our project planner."

"You guys get started without me," Rachel says. "I wanna go network a little."

"Networking is for people who haven't found their team members yet," I say. "We should use this time to our advantage by getting started on our project."

She's already standing up, though, sloth in hand. "I won't be long. I just wanna make a few connections. By the time I leave here tomorrow, I bet I'll have at least a hundred new followers."

As she saunters off, I grind my teeth to keep from saying something snarky. When she's out of earshot, I say, "Well, I guess we'll build this app without her."

I expect at least a little commiseration from my teammates. After all, Rachel abandoned us to go build her already substantial ZigZag following. But Christine either didn't hear me or is pretending she didn't, and Jason's giving me a serious scowl.

"What?" I say, instantly on the defensive.

"Why are you being so rude?" he says.

"Because I think she should be *here*, working with us. Not off increasing her follower count."

"Nah, it started before that," he says. "You just don't like her."

"That's not true!" It's totally true.

"Can you guys stop bickering?" Christine says. She sounds exasperated. "We're wasting time. Besides, maybe she'll come back with good intel. It can't hurt to find out what some of the other teams are up to. Let's just focus on starting this project."

She's right, of course. I shouldn't be letting Rachel upset

me. I should be focused on my goal, and the things I can control. Like my contribution. My efforts. My work.

With that in mind, I ignore Jason's comment and dive right into the design phase of the project. The three of us come up with plans for what the app should look like and how it should function, drawing diagrams for each different screen. I'm so blissfully lost in the work, I almost forget about Rachel's existence, until she sashays back to our table a little while later.

"How's it going?" she asks.

"All right," Christine says, handing her the notebook we're using to sketch up sample screens. "We've put together some preliminary mock-ups."

Rachel gives the pictures a cursory glance, says, "Looks good," then starts scrolling through her phone.

"Get any new followers?" Christine's tone is slightly mocking, but Rachel doesn't pick up on it. She simply says, "Mmhmm," without ever looking away from her screen.

"How did you get so many followers in the first place?" Christine asks.

Finally, Rachel puts down her phone. "I don't know. It just sort of happened. I guess I make interesting content."

I know exactly how she got so many followers. Last year, she posted a short video of herself doing a dance she called "The Spice Rack," involving a lot of shoulder popping and arm waves, set to the tune of some old Spice Girls song. Admittedly, it looked supercool (just like everything Rachel touches) and then it went viral. Not "Gangnam Style" kind of viral. Just a *little* viral. Enough to get her several thousand new followers.

Thing is, she didn't come up with that dance. A freshman, Jameela Davis, came up with it. Jameela had posted it to Zig-Zag, but no one really paid attention. A couple of weeks later, though, Rachel copied the dance, posted it to *her* ZigZag, and that's when it suddenly blew up. Some people at school called her out on it, and eventually Rachel gave Jameela credit, but by then the collective internet had moved on to the next viral video. No one cared about the dance anymore. They didn't care that Rachel had stolen it, either.

So if Rachel's ZigZag content is considered interesting, it's only because she's ripping it off of other people.

"Really, though," she says, "it's just about luck. You post the right thing at the right time and it happens to catch on and suddenly you've gone viral! And I know Jason's *totally* on the verge of going viral himself." She reaches across the table and squeezes the back of his hand. "Keep posting awesome content and soon you'll get that one big video that'll shoot you right to the top of ZigZag's Trending page."

Jason's eyes flash to me, his face beet red, before he turns his attention back to his laptop and starts typing away.

"Can I have your attention please?" James Lee is back at the podium, full of enthusiasm as per usual. "Hi again, everybody! I hope you've all had a chance to discuss the possibilities with your teammates and have identified potential solutions to your biggest problems! Now it's time to start building your prototypes!

"In just a few minutes, we'll be setting up interactive workshops in the classrooms down the hall. These will help you answer any technical questions you may have about the ZigZag API or app development in general. For more specific information about each workshop, check out the schedule printed in your hackathon brochure."

I flip open the pamphlet and find the workshop schedule. "There are a lot of good ones here. I'm not sure which one to go to."

"Maybe we should split up," Jason says. "Each of us can go to a different one and report back to the team."

Rachel peruses her pamphlet, then tosses it on the table. "I'm gonna opt out."

My jaw is so tightly clenched, I may crack a molar. "What do you mean, 'opt out'?"

"These are all technical workshops. I don't really consider myself a techie. I'm more of an idea person."

There are a lot of things I want to say right now. But I shouldn't say them. Christine will tell me I'm wasting time, and Jason will call me rude. Rachel won't care what I have to say, either. With fewer than fifty ZigZag followers, my opinion is irrelevant.

I slap my laptop closed and stand up. "Well, *I'm* a techie, so I'm going to a workshop."

I speedwalk to the exit. Christine calls behind me, "Ashley, wait up!" but I keep on going. This cavernous room suddenly feels cramped. I need to get out.

In the hallway, there's a poster propped on an easel with the times and locations of the workshops. I stand in front of it, staring at the words without actually processing any information. It's hard to focus with all these feelings swirling around inside my brain. I'm angry, I'm frustrated, I'm scared. But mostly, I'm sad.

Suddenly, there's a hand on my shoulder. Christine's by my side, and she doesn't look happy. "Come with me."

She drags me by the arm down the hallway, around the corner, and into an empty stairwell. As soon as the door clicks shut behind us, she says, "What is going on with you?"

"Nothing."

"Then why are you acting so mean toward Rachel?"

"Because she's the most annoying person on the planet."

"She's not my favorite person, either, but she *is* on our team and she has good ideas, so we have to work together now. You being snarky doesn't help us get any closer to first place."

"I'm sorry." It's true. My attitude isn't helping our team.

She lets out an irritated sigh. "Heaven told me this would happen."

"What do you mean?"

"I'll let her explain."

I'm not sure how that's going to happen when Heaven's in Puerto Rico with her grandma right now. But then Christine whips out her phone and starts tapping the screen, and all of a sudden there's Heaven's face.

"Tell her what you told me yesterday," Christine says.

"I said you shouldn't let Rachel join your team," Heaven says. "It's blowing up in your face now, isn't it?"

"What are you talking about?" I am so confused.

Heaven says, "When Jason asked Christine if Rachel could join your team, I told her to tell him no. I knew having her around would make you upset."

"Why?"

"Because I know you don't like her. You were so snippy when I asked about her dating Jason the other day."

"Well, she's infuriating. I mean, you have to see what she's doing right now, Heaven. Wandering around the room, trying to get more ZigZag followers. She's not contributing anything to the team."

"Oh, okay." Heaven nods. "It wouldn't have anything to do with the fact that she and Jason are together, though, would it?"

"No, of course not." The words don't sound convincing, even to my own ears.

"Do you have a thing for Jason?" Christine asks. "Heaven told me you do, but I didn't believe her."

When I don't answer, Heaven says, "I knew it."

"Dammit," Christine says. "I should've listened to you. I'm sorry, Ashley. I didn't think she was right."

"Does he know how you feel?" Heaven asks. "Like, have you ever had a conversation about being more than friends?"

"No."

"Then why don't you talk to him about it? Clear the air."

I shake my head. "I can't. It's too late now. He's back together with Rachel."

Christine takes a deep breath and blows it out slowly. "Look, I know this must suck for you, but we only have a few hours left to win this hackathon. And if you want this internship at ZigZag, you need to set aside your feelings for Jason and focus. Now."

In that moment, with Christine's eyes piercing mine, I realize how profoundly stupid I'm being. I'm dragging my best friend—and my future—down because I'm letting my feelings get the best of me. And though I may not be able to control how I feel, I can control how I react to those feelings.

So I walk out of that stairwell with a vow to work well with Rachel. Even if it tears me up inside.

Chapter Twenty-Five

I keep my vow.

No matter how many times Rachel mentions her tremendous ZigZag following or flirts with Jason, I stay focused on our goal: to get a working prototype of this outfit crowdsourcing app—which we've tentatively titled Shop My Closet—up and running before the demos start tomorrow morning.

Unfortunately, it's not looking good.

As we get down to coding, we quickly discover we're in over our heads. Letting users link to retailers and tracing those sales back to ZigZag is a lot more complicated than we thought it would be. There's no way we can finish this in twenty-four hours, especially since Christine and I are the only ones doing any significant coding. While Jason is staying true to his word and taking the whole endeavor seriously, he's still new to this, so he can't handle some of the more complicated code.

And Rachel's barely doing anything at all. She's not even spending much time at our table. Whenever I look up from my computer screen, she's wandering around the conference hall, undoubtedly collecting more followers.

We work nonstop until dinner, which we scarf down in the dining hall before reconvening around our laptops at seven o'clock. Well, at least three of us reconvene. Rachel's completely MIA. Though it's not like she'd be contributing anything significant even if she *was* here.

"Let's see what we've got left to do," I say, trying my best to keep a positive attitude. When I pull up our virtual project planner, though, my positive attitude starts to crumble. Our "Finished" column is practically empty, while our "To Do" column is completely full.

Christine says what we're all thinking. "I don't see how we can possibly finish this."

"Are there any tasks we can abandon? Like, things that are nice-to-have, but not essential for the app to function?"

"Not really," she says. "If we want to present them with something that actually works, we've gotta do all of this."

There's nothing else to say but "Ugh."

Maybe it's time to give up. We don't stand a chance of winning this competition. Which shouldn't be such a surprise, really. ZigZag already told me I wasn't good enough for their summer internship program. I should've taken the hint when I got that rejection letter.

I'm about to shut down my laptop in defeat when Mr. P approaches our table. "Hey there," he says, all smiles. I'd be happy to see him if I weren't presently coming to terms with the fact that my entire life is an abysmal failure.

Still, I smile back. "Hey, Mr. P."

"How's it going? Making good progress on your prototype?"

I can't bring myself to answer. Instead, Christine says, "We're kind of stuck, actually."

Mr. P crouches down next to us. "Tell me what's going on."

We show him our diagrams, our requirements documents, our plans for designing the app. He reviews it all, and after a moment of silent thought, he asks, "What made you decide on this particular project?"

"What do you mean?" I ask.

"Well, why did you choose to write a shopping app? That's basically what this is, right?"

"We thought the judges might like it," Christine says. "You know, since it's something that can help ZigZag make money."

He scratches his chin. "My advice to you is to worry less about what the judges want to see and more about what you want to create. The whole purpose of the hackathon is to build something you believe in. Genuine enthusiasm fuels innovation. Create a project you're passionate about and the judges will see that passion shine through."

I think of all the time I've spent at Coding Club. Hours of writing and testing code; trying and failing over and over and over again; never giving up until I find a solution to my problem. I don't put in all that hard work because I want to impress anyone. I do it because it means something to me. Because it's interesting and challenging and, of course, fun.

Fun is what motivates anybody who really loves to code. Fun inspired my light-up hoodie and Jason's fart app. It's what should be inspiring us now. This shopping app, though? It's not fun. But there *is* an idea I'm actually enthusiastic about. One that I can definitely pour some passion into.

"There's this other idea we were considering," I say. "A decision-making app that hooks into ZigZag's API. One that lets you crowdsource advice from your friends. That way, when you need suggestions or encouragement, you can reach out to them for help."

"It sounds like an interesting concept," Mr. P says. "Is it something you believe in?"

"Yes, absolutely." I turn to Christine and Jason. "What do you guys think?"

Christine says, "I love the idea, but we can't shift gears this late in the game. We're running out of time."

"We can totally do it. I know how to make it work. There's so much code we've already written that we can reuse."

"Well, let's do it, then," Christine says. "Jason, you in?"

"Sure." He nods, but the corner of his lip twitches the tiniest bit, so I know he's not totally convinced. Probably because we're ditching his girlfriend's idea.

Still, the relief I feel is palpable. "Thank you so much, Mr. P."

"You're welcome. I think you have a really strong chance of winning." He lowers his voice, then says, "Between you and me, your team has some of the best coders in the room."

I don't know if he really means it or if he's just saying it to boost our spirits, but his little pep talk springs us into action. As soon as he leaves, Christine and I divvy up the work, assigning Jason some of the smaller, less complicated tasks. We don't bother giving Rachel anything, since she's nowhere to be seen.

Regardless, a fresh wave of positivity has washed over our team. Together, the three of us can accomplish anything. Even winning this hackathon!

At least, that's how I feel until Rachel comes back. She plops down next to me and asks, "How's it going?"

"We've decided to switch gears," Christine says.

"How so?"

"We're not doing Shop My Closet anymore. We're going back to Ashley's original idea, the decision-making app."

"Um, no." Rachel says it like there's no room for debate. "We need to do something that'll capture the judges' attention."

"This will capture the judges' attention," I say. My voice is calm, which requires a very big effort on my part.

"No, it won't. Why did you make this decision without consulting me?"

She cannot be serious. "Because you weren't around."

"I'm still a member of this team." She narrows her eyes, clearly miffed that we didn't send out a search party to reel her in.

Before I can say something snarky in response, Jason mercifully interjects. "Look, the shopping app was a good idea, but it's way too much work for such a short period of time. Christine and Ashley are the only two experienced coders here. They can't handle it all on their own."

Her lips spread into a wide, sly smile. "So why don't we enlist a little help."

"What does that mean?"

She looks over her shoulder, checking to see if anyone's listening in, then leans in close. "I've been talking to some other teams, and it looks like a lot of people are actually using code libraries they've found on the internet. Samples and snippets other people have posted online."

"You mean, they're cheating," I say.

"Yes," she says, slowly, like I'm having difficulty understanding her. "But if everybody else is doing it, then why can't we?"

"Because it's against the rules," Christine says.

"So? If you think we can win this hackathon by playing by the rules, then you're delusional. Other people are turning out really cool projects, and they're not bothering to play by the rules. We'll never beat them unless we go with our original design."

"There's not enough time to go with our original design," Jason says.

"Which is why I'm telling you we need to enlist help."

"I repeat: that's cheating." My voice is so loud, people at the next table turn to gawk.

Rachel's eyes are daggers, but I keep talking, anyway. "Maybe you're fine with stealing stuff that other people made and passing it off as your own, but we can't do that here. Not if we want to win fairly."

"I'm not sure why you think we should be listening to you," she says. "You don't know what ZigZag wants."

"We shouldn't be concerned with what ZigZag wants to see. We should be concerned about what we want to create. My follower count is totally irrelevant here."

"I'm not talking about your follower count. Though, you're right, it's pretty pathetic."

"Come on, Rachel," Jason says, a warning in his voice.

A tingling sensation emerges at the base of my spine. It travels upward, crawling along my vertebrae, until it reaches the back of my neck. I'm not sure I want to know what she means, but part of me is certain that I already do.

"No, seriously," she says. "They already rejected you from their internship program."

Jason says, "Rachel, enough."

But she keeps on going. "Why are you dictating what the team is doing when you're so obviously not what ZigZag is looking for?"

"Enough!" Jason yells, but Rachel's smiling this Cheshire

cat smile. So smug. So self-righteous. She knows she's got me cornered. This time, I don't have a snappy comeback.

The tingling in my body has spread now, up into my scalp and across my forehead and around my throat. It's hard to think or speak or breathe. I stand up and walk away before the hot tears spill down my cheeks.

There are way too many people in this building. People on laptops, people in sleeping bags, people talking and planning and coding and cheating. Every corner of the conference room is occupied, the hallways are busy. And right now, I need a little privacy.

I run down the hall and around the corner, where the stairwell is blissfully empty. Then I sit down on the bottom step and I cry.

These past couple of weeks have been the hardest weeks of my life. I lost out on the internship, I lost my mother's trust, I lost faith in my future and tore my goals to shreds. I dated the guy of my dreams, only to discover he wasn't the guy of my dreams at all. And the *real* guy of my dreams, the guy I'm in love with? He doesn't love me back.

Now I know for sure he doesn't love me back. Because if he loved me, he wouldn't have told Rachel that I was rejected from ZigZag, when he knew it was one of the biggest disappointments of my life. I picture them laughing, talking about how pathetic I am, and the sobs come faster and harder.

Then the stairwell doorknob turns, and the door slowly creaks open. I'm fully expecting Christine to walk in, but my breath catches when I see who it is.

Jason.

Frazzled, I jump to my feet. "What are you doing here?"

"I wanted to check on you." He takes one look at my swollen, tear-strewn face and says, "Are you okay?"

"No, I'm not okay. Why did you tell her about my rejection?"

"I thought it would help motivate her."

"Motivate her to what, humiliate me?"

"Of course not! I thought if she knew how important this internship was to you, how much was at stake, she would work hard and try her best."

"She doesn't care about what's important to me. You heard her, she thinks I'm pathetic."

"She just said that because she's jealous."

"Jealous of what?"

"Of you."

"That's ridiculous. There's nothing for her to be jealous of."

"Really? You're smart, you're funny, you're pretty"—*I'm pretty?*—"and the thing that kills her the most is you're original. You'd never steal someone else's stuff to get ahead."

Is he talking about the code she wanted to steal to win the hackathon? Or the dance she stole that made her go viral? Either way, "She's the worst. I can't believe you brought her here."

Jason's face goes dark, like a cloud settled over him. "You know, you're not the only person in the world who has feelings."

"I don't care about Rachel's feelings."

"I'm not talking about Rachel. I'm talking about me."

"Oh, gee, sorry I'm insulting your girlfriend." My voice drips with sarcasm. "Of course you had to bring her. How could you possibly survive for twenty-four hours without her by your side?"

"She's not my girlfriend."

"Yeah, right. I saw her cameo in your latest video."

"That doesn't mean we're together."

"Then why have you been hanging around with her so much?"

"Because I needed to distract myself."

"Distract yourself from what?"

"From you!"

This is ridiculous. "Why on earth would you need to distract yourself from me?"

"You know, for someone so smart, you're really freakin' obtuse." He presses the heels of his palms into his eye sockets and lets loose with a sound that's halfway between a growl and a groan.

Then he lowers his hands and looks at me with his brown eyes and says, "I'm in love with you, Ashley. I've been in love with you for . . . I don't know how long. Every stupid thing I've ever done has been to get your attention. To make you laugh or to smile or to think I was cool. To tell you how I feel without really telling you. Remember that prank on the bus?"

I conjure the image of the cartoon cat, eyes closed tightly and hugging a pink heart. HI, I THINK YOU'RE CUTE.

"Yeah. That was for you. But I was too chicken to send it *only* to you, so I sent it to everyone on the B9. Which turned out to be a really bad idea."

My head is spinning. Back then, I hadn't yet realized I loved him. Though, deep down, I've probably always loved him. Even in the second grade, when he was torturing Ms. Chen with his rubber tarantula.

"After that," he continues, "I realized it was pointless because you were already dating someone else. Do you know how hard it's been for me, knowing you're going out with Walker Beech? I even got that stupid cologne he wears because I thought you might like it."

"For the record," I say, "please don't ever wear that again. And I'm not going out with Walker. Not anymore."

"Oh." He releases a heavy breath. "Anyway, that's why I started hanging out with Rachel again. I figured if I couldn't make you love me, then I could make myself fall in love with her. But it didn't work. You can't make yourself feel something you don't."

I take two steps toward him, closing the enormous gap between us. "You can't make me love you, Jason."

"Yeah, I already said that."

"No. I mean, you can't make me love you because I already do."

The cloud hanging over him has suddenly blown away. His face brightens, his cheeks flush. There's a subtle glimmer in his eyes. It's a glimmer I know well.

"Are you serious?" he asks.

"Yes. I love you. I think I always have."

I take his hands in mine. They're warm and electric. We twine our fingers together and I can feel his touch up and down the length of my arms. I feel it all the way down to my bones.

"I don't understand," he says. "Why didn't you say anything?"

"I thought you were back with Rachel."

"This is crazy."

"Is it, though? We have so much in common. We've known each other forever. I feel like we could be perfect together. Don't you?"

"Absolutely." He reaches one hand up to cradle my face, his

thumb gently stroking my cheek. "You know, every time we're together now, all I can think about is what it would be like to kiss you. Do you think it would be okay if—"

I don't even let him finish the question. In an instant, my mouth is on his, and it's definitely no chaste peck on the lips. It's explosive and brilliant—confetti cannons and fireworks and Times Square on New Year's Eve, all at the same time. Yet there's a strange sense of comfort, too. Like all paths have been leading me to this moment, right here, with this boy.

This is what a real First Kiss should be like. And I know I don't have much experience, but I can confidently say this is the most perfect First Kiss in the history of First Kisses.

Our kiss deepens and intensifies, and we wrap our arms around each other like we're holding on for dear life. It feels so good, I don't want to let go.

But then I remember where we are. In a stairwell, at the hackathon. The seconds are ticking by, and I've got to keep my eyes on the prize.

As hard as it is, I break the most perfect First Kiss in the history of First Kisses.

"There'll be plenty of time for this later," I say. "Right now, we've got a hackathon to win."

Chapter Twenty-Six

As we walk back to the conference hall, Jason tries to hold my hand, but I'm too nervous about facing Rachel. If she sees us strolling in together looking all dreamy and in love, who knows what she'd say or do? Maybe she'd start some rumor. Maybe she'd even be spiteful enough to derail our project.

Though I'm sure she's dying to win that internship. Working for ZigZag would undoubtedly send her follower count through the roof.

Either way, I need to be strategic. The PDA can wait until after we take first place.

Christine's sitting alone at the table, tapping away at her keyboard. When we sit down, she doesn't break her stride or look away from the screen.

"Where's Rachel?" I ask.

Her tapping stops abruptly. "She quit."

"She quit the hackathon?"

"No, she quit our team." Christine twists around in her seat and points to the other end of the room, where Rachel's taking a selfie. "She joined those guys in the corner. I guess they were a team of three and somehow she weaseled her way in."

"Can she switch teams this late in the game?" Jason asks.

"I don't know, but either way, I'm pretty sure Rachel doesn't care about the rules," Christine says. "When I told her in no uncertain terms that we weren't going to steal code from the internet, she called me a priss. Then I called her something that I don't want to repeat. Anyway, she said she's here to win and that there's another team that's been asking her to join them. So she took her sloth and huffed away."

Wow. "So it's just the three of us now?"

"Yes. To be honest, it's for the best. She's not doing anything for us." She looks over at Jason. "Sorry, I know she's your friend."

"She's not my friend," Jason says. "Let's not stress about her anymore. We've got work to do."

Christine nods, then shifts her gaze back to me. "Are you okay?"

Mere moments ago, I thought I'd never be okay. Now I feel better than okay. "I feel great."

"Great! Then let's get down to business."

The three of us work long into the night. While Christine and I write code, Jason runs tests. Our prototype isn't perfect, but it's coming together. Sure, I'd like it to be a bit snazzier, but this competition isn't about style or sparkle, it's about technical skill. And we have that in spades. Mr. P said it himself: we're some of the best coders in the room.

By three in the morning, my eyelids are so heavy, I can barely keep them open. But I can't give in to sleep, there's too much to do. While Christine and Jason go off to take power naps, I push through to the morning, fueled by adrenaline and ambition. And also, like, five cans of Coke.

Hours later, I'm exhausted, drained, and completely spent. I have no idea what time it is, and I've also never felt a greater sense of accomplishment. Every item on the to-do list is crossed off. The prototype is working. Our project is complete. No cheating necessary.

I'm reviewing the code, cleaning up any unused variables and adding explanatory comments, when Jason returns with a bowl of fruit and a muffin. "Grabbed these from the breakfast buffet for you. Figured you might be hungry."

I didn't think I was hungry, but one look at this food and I'm suddenly ravenous, tearing into the muffin as if I haven't eaten for days. "Thank you," I say. "Where's Christine?"

"In the dining hall. She's been talking to some guy she said she went to camp with. They look like they're into each other. Are they dating?"

"Not yet."

Right on cue, Christine appears, her face flushed and smiling. I raise my eyebrows in her direction and she freezes. "What?"

"How's Ahmad?"

"Fine. More important, how's the prototype?"

"It's done!" I slide my laptop over so they can see my screen. "Check it out."

Christine scrolls through the code and clicks through the app. "This looks great, Ashley. The judges are gonna be so impressed."

My gaze slides over to the corner, where Rachel is sitting with her new teammates. They look confident. Like they've got this competition in the bag.

"What if Rachel's right?" I ask. "What if this isn't as good as the other teams who are using borrowed code?"

"They're not 'using borrowed code,'" Christine says. "They're cheating. And that's objectively wrong."

"Well, should we say something to someone about it?"

"No," Jason says. "If we go around lobbing accusations, it'll throw the competition into chaos. And if the judges can't find proof they were cheating, it'll make us look like bad competitors."

"We're doing the right thing," Christine says. "We just have to trust that it'll work out in our favor."

She's right. We need to win fairly. Even though nothing about this situation seems fair.

"Can I have your attention please?" James Lee is back on the microphone, enthusiastic as ever. "It's 11:59, which means everyone needs to stop what they're doing and submit their projects for consideration!"

It's now or never. "Are we ready?"

Christine and Jason both nod.

Here goes nothing.

I pull up the hackathon website, upload our code, and hope for the best.

"In a few moments," James says, "we'll begin calling up teams one by one to present the demos of your prototypes to our panel of judges. Due to the large number of participants, we kindly ask you to limit your presentation to a maximum of five minutes! Please choose *one* team member to be the presenter! And don't forget to listen carefully for your names to be called!"

Oh no. We haven't chosen a presenter. "Who should do the talking?"

Without hesitating, Christine says, "You, obviously. This is your chance to woo the judges. To show them how badass you are."

"But I didn't do this alone. We worked as a team. Together."

"Yeah, but this means the most to you," Christine says. "Look, even if we win first place, you know I'm not gonna take that internship. My parents already sent in the nonrefundable deposit for my summer study program at Yale. There's no way I'm giving that up now."

My eyes flash to Jason. "What about you? Do you want to present?"

"No way," he says. "I'm still a noob. You can explain things way better than I can."

Well, that settles it. I'm going to stand up in front of a panel of ZigZag employees and present this hackathon project all by myself.

The presentations are done privately, so only the teams and the judges can hear what's going on. I'm immensely relieved about this, because I can't imagine staring out at a sea of hundreds of faces while attempting to give a coherent demo of our prototype. Coding is my strength. Public speaking? Not so much.

Still, I'm feeling positive, especially after I do a few practice runs for Christine and Jason. Once I've memorized every word I'm going to say, there's nothing left to do but sit and wait.

Team after team is called up to the front of the room, where the judges are sitting at the dais, taking notes. I study each judge's face, trying to commit them all to memory, thinking maybe one of them will wind up being my manager this summer.

I wonder how many people in this room are doing the same thing. How many of them want this internship as badly as I do?

"Do you think most people here want to be software engineers one day?" I ask to no one in particular.

"You know I don't," Christine says.

"You don't?" Jason says. "But you're so good at it."

"I mean, it's fun, but I don't wanna make a career out of it."

"Do you know what you want to do, then?"

"I'd like to work in public health. Research infectious diseases and help prevent pandemics. That kind of thing. What about you?"

His lip twitches slightly. "I'm not sure. Honestly, I haven't spent much time thinking about it. I like coding, but I don't really know enough about it yet to say whether I wanna be a software engineer or anything."

"You picked it up quickly," I say. "Do you think you'll stick with it?"

"Yeah, I want to, but . . ." He hesitates, then says, "I've actually been thinking about changing up my YouTube channel. The pranking thing's been done, you know? At this point, I'm just recycling old gags. It's getting old. But what if I started doing coding tutorials? You know, for noobs like me. You guys were amazing teachers and everything, but I gotta be honest, sometimes it was a little intimidating to learn from geniuses. I want to be the guy who's learning to code alongside people. Teaching and learning at the same time."

It's an ingenious concept, and Jason's so great in front of the camera, too. He'll really make his tutorials entertaining. "That sounds so cool. What kind of stuff are you thinking of teaching?"

He shrugs. "I might start with a walk-through of how to build the digital fart button."

"Pranking and coding, together at last," I say. "I can't wait to see it."

Jason smiles at me, his eyes glimmering, and there's nothing I want more than to kiss him again, right here, right now. But then James Lee's enthusiastic voice booms through the speakers: "Can we have Ashley Bergen, Jason Eisler, and Christine Kong to the front of the room, please?"

This is it. The big presentation. The moment that could change my life forever.

No pressure or anything.

We grab our laptops and weave around the crowded tables, avoiding eye contact with other nervous participants. As we walk, I hear Christine and Jason whispering words of encouragement.

"You've got this."

"We're gonna rock it."

I hope they're right.

At the front of the room, the four judges are seated at the dais, along with the hackathon organizer, Professor Osman. She's the only one smiling; everyone else looks absolutely emotionless. Even James Lee, the king of the exclamation point, is stone-faced. I guess this is part of their strategy, so we don't know what they're really thinking.

I connect my laptop to the Smart TV on which everyone is doing their demos. Then I take a deep breath and make eye contact with each of the judges, these people who control my fate. They don't know who I am or what I'm truly capable of. This presentation doesn't really define me. But I'm still gonna give it my all.

And whatever happens, I'll never give up on my dreams.

Chapter Twenty-Seven

The presentation is a total blur. I don't remember what I've said or what I've done. All I know is the prototype works like it's supposed to, and the judges remain poker-faced throughout.

Sometimes it's hard to keep going without any real-time feedback. Are they bored? Unimpressed? Are they even paying attention? Their tight-lipped stares remind me of that glazed-over look Walker always had when I was explaining logarithmic functions. Like these judges don't care whether I win or lose. They just want me to wrap it up already so they can go home.

The important thing is, I get through it. And when I'm done, Christine and Jason can't contain their excitement.

"You nailed it!"

"That was perfect."

I hope they're right.

We sit off to the side while the remaining teams go through their presentations. The adrenaline rush has subsided, leaving us wordless and worn out. But my ears perk up when James Lee announces, "Can we have Daniel Lim, Max Anderson,

Harrison Murphy, and Rachel Gibbons up to the front of the room, please?"

From across the conference hall, I see her topknot pop up alongside three guys in button-down shirts. They walk over to the dais, and while one of the boys connects his laptop to the Smart TV, Rachel starts talking. She's clearly the presenter. The lively lilt of her voice carries all the way back here. And even though I can't make out exactly what she's saying, it's clear the judges are eating it up. Their normally stoic faces are smiling. One of them actually laughs.

I'm doomed.

Jason catches me staring and says, "Don't sweat it. She might be putting on a good show, but I'm sure it's all style, no substance."

"Or the substance is stolen," Christine adds.

When their presentation is over, Rachel does a little curtsy, like she's some sort of debutante. After her team takes their seats, James Lee approaches the podium.

"Can I have your attention, please?" A hush falls over the room. "We've seen everyone's presentations and, boy, are we excited about the cutting-edge, innovative ideas you've shared with us today!" Applause breaks out, then dies down. "We're going to tally up our scores now, and we'll be back to announce the winning teams in just a moment!"

The wait is excruciating. Each second feels like a minute, each minute feels like an hour. Time is going by so slowly, I swear I can actually feel the hair growing on my legs. My fingers tap a nervous drumbeat on the table, until Jason reaches out to squeeze my hand. His touch calms me down, slows my heart rate, eases my breathing.

Until James stands up and taps the microphone. Then I can't breathe at all.

"The judges have made our final decision! Without further ado, I give you the winners of the New York City High School Spring Break Hackathon, sponsored by ZigZag Technologies Inc.! Third place goes to Goran Marasovic, Ameet Choudhary, and Reginald Walker, for their app, ZigZag Dance Revolution!"

The room applauds and I clap along half-heartedly as the third-place winners claim their drones.

"I wonder what that app's all about," Jason says.

"Probably makes it easier for people to steal dances from each other," Christine says.

If it were possible for a person to die from anticipation, I'd be lying lifeless on the floor right now. My future hangs in the balance. Will I spend the summer as a ZigZag intern in Silicon Valley, or will I continue to bag groceries at the ShopRite in Brooklyn?

My heart's in my throat as the applause fades and James announces, "Our second-place winners are Ashley Bergen, Christine Kong, and Jason Eisler, for their app, Decisions Decisions!"

We didn't win the internship. I'll be spending my summer in Brooklyn. My future has been decided.

I feel like a zombie, walking up to the dais to claim my Smartwatch. What do I even need this thing for? It's completely useless.

Jason puts his hand on the small of my back, but it does little to comfort me. Christine's standing to my right, her eyes full of regret. She mouths "Sorry," and I inhale deeply to keep from crying.

"Finally," James announces, "our first-place winners—and new summer interns for ZigZag—are Daniel Lim, Max Anderson, Harrison Murphy, and Rachel Gibbons, for their incredibly innovative shopping app, ZigZag-A-LamaDingDong!"

Rachel's high-pitched squeal rises above the riotous applause as she leads the group of button-down boys to the dais. They're given laptops and more ZigZag swag, and they pose for pictures with the judges. The judges who will be their managers this summer. Because they're all going to Silicon Valley.

"ZigZag-A-LamaDingDong?" Jason's voice oozes with disgust. "What kind of stupid name is that?"

"I guess ZigZag really did want a shopping app," Christine says. "We can still report them for cheating, you know."

Jason turns to me. "It's true, we can. You deserve this internship, Ashley."

They're both looking at me now, like the decision is all mine to make. I glance over at Rachel and the whole ZigZag-A-LamaDingDong team. They're chatting with the judges now, who are laughing and smiling. They seem to really like her. Maybe she'll fit in well in their office. Maybe they don't care about a little cheating, anyway.

This is the second time I've lost out on this internship, and I can't help but think the universe is trying to tell me something: this internship wasn't meant for me. I tried my very best, but like Jason said, I can't force things to go my way all the time. Besides, it's just one summer program. It doesn't define who I am or what I'm capable of or how much I'm worth.

"What do you want to do, Ashley?" Christine asks.

"I want to move on with my life." The moment I say it, I know I mean it. There'll be other opportunities, other chances to prove myself. And maybe one day ZigZag will realize they made a huge mistake by letting me go.

We return to our table, Smartwatches in tow, and start gathering up our belongings. As I'm stuffing my laptop into my backpack, I see Mr. P standing at the front of the room. He's talking to Professor Osman with this big energy, all hand-waving and head nods. Then he points toward us and starts walking our way.

"Congratulations!" Mr. P says. "Great job winning second place!"

It's funny: I've been moping and complaining about not coming in first, never acknowledging exactly how awesome it is to come in second. There are hundreds of people in this room who would've killed to be in our shoes. And we didn't have to cheat to get here.

"Thanks," I say.

"I want to introduce you all to Professor Osman," he says. "Professor Osman, these are some of my best students. Christine and Ashley have been part of our school's Coding Club all year and have been developing very advanced projects, and although Jason's just getting started, he's really demonstrated a great aptitude for the subject."

Jason's cheeks are bright red. It must feel nice for a teacher to praise him instead of putting him down.

"It's lovely to meet you." Professor Osman shakes our hands in turn. "I had a chance to review your code, and I have to say, I was very impressed with your work."

Instantly, Jason points to me and Christine. "That was all these two. They're the brains behind this operation. I just did whatever they told me to do."

"Thank you for your honesty," she says. "I'm here because Mr. Podonsky says you've been working on wearables in your club recently."

"Yes," I say. "I made a light-up hoodie that responds to music."

"And I made a temperature-sensitive pendant," Christine says.

"That's wonderful. My research lab here at NYU is focused on creating wearable body sensors, with the hopes of improving modern healthcare. We're looking for an intern to join us this summer, to help us review data while learning more about the field. He said one or both of you might be interested?"

You know that old saying *When one door closes, another opens*? Right now, I feel like I'm standing in front of a window, and my future is right on the other side.

I'm screaming on the inside, but somehow I manage to answer her calmly. "I am absolutely interested."

"Wonderful. I'll connect with Mr. Podonsky over the next few days and we can set up some time for a chat."

"Great. I can have him send over my transcript, if you'd like."

She shakes her head. "That won't be necessary. I've known Mr. Podonsky since college, and I respect his opinion immensely. You come highly recommended. I'd just like to talk to you a little bit more. Get to know you. Then we can see if my lab is the right fit."

With that, she shakes our hands again, and walks off with Mr. P.

"Um . . ." Christine swivels around, her eyes wide and excited. "I kind of can't believe how perfect that was."

"Me neither," I say.

"You're definitely gonna get that internship in her lab," Jason says. "She said she didn't even need to see your transcript."

"Yeah. But you know what? If it doesn't work out, then it probably just wasn't meant for me."

Jason takes my hand and gives it a little squeeze. His eyes are glimmering, and I realize I'm taking home the best prize of all.

Someone calls Christine's name from across the room. I glance over to see Ahmad waving and smiling in her direction. She hoists her backpack onto her shoulders and says, "I'm gonna grab a late lunch with Ahmad." When I raise my eyebrows, she says, "It's not like that."

"Okay. But just so you know, I think he seems super fantastic and totally mature."

"He really is." She gets this dreamy look I've never seen before. It suits her. "Anyway, Ashley, you wanna hang out tonight? Heaven's plane should be landing any second and she's coming over to my place at seven o'clock."

"Sure!" Oh, wait. "Actually, I can't. I'm grounded. Mom's got me on lockdown for the rest of spring break."

"Bummer. But at least it's only one more day."

That's right. On Monday morning, I'll be back at school.

My epic spring break is almost over.

Chapter Twenty-Eight

When Mom sees the Smartwatch, she's completely overjoyed. "I want you to wear this at all times!" she says, like the total stalker she is.

Admittedly, the watch *is* kind of cool. Mom's obviously only excited about the GPS capabilities, but there's also a compass and a pedometer and a heart rate monitor. I already have ideas for apps I can write to take advantage of all these cool features. Which makes me even more excited about the possibility of working this summer in a lab that's focused on developing wearables.

I spend all night in my room, texting with Jason, who's in his room, one floor below mine. Being grounded sucks, I'm not gonna lie. But it's nice to be able to flick my wrist and connect with the guy I love.

I'm also working on a project: rebuilding my vision board. Mom's right—I need new dreams to work toward. So I collect some images that fit this new vision of my future. The NYU logo, photos of the New York City skyline, a selfie of me and

Jason that I snapped on the subway ride home from the hack-athon.

Only one vestige of my old vision board makes the cut. An inspirational phrase: *The best is yet to come.* Because I truly believe it.

While I'm putting it together, Dad sends me a text: *Home from the Bahamas. I'd like to talk to you about what happened the other night, and what you said. I really do care about you, Ashley. Can we get breakfast next weekend? I promise not to flake this time.*

I'm not sure if I believe he won't flake, but I reply *Sure,* because it's nice to see him putting in the effort. For the first time I can remember, he actually listened to what I said. Maybe the tiny little girl in my head is right. Maybe he's capable of change, after all.

The next day is Sunday. My last day of spring break. I'm allowed to leave the house, but only to go to work. Jason picks me up, so Mom isn't worried about who I'm with or where I'm going.

We hold hands as we walk to ShopRite together, the same route we always take. Left on Sixty-First Street, right on Twenty-First Avenue. This neighborhood hasn't changed much since we were kids. Yet, somehow, everything looks different. The streets are brighter, rosier, full of promise. Anything's possible now that I know Jason Eisler loves me.

We don't walk home together, though. I've gotta swing by Party City and I don't want him to know. Because today is April 10. Jason's *real* birthday. I duck out of work a few minutes early and text him as I walk to the store: *Got something special planned. Will call you soon.* 💜

I rush home as soon as I'm done buying what I need, then send Jason a text from the front of our building: *Meet me outside.*

My watch buzzes with his reply: *be down in 5.*

I used to think that glimmer in Jason's eyes meant he was up to no good. But though his pranks get him in trouble, they still manage to lighten the mood and make people smile, even if just for a moment. And couldn't we all stand to have a little more fun? After all, we only get one run through high school. Might as well make the most of it.

Through the glass doors, I see Jason emerge from the elevator. Time to get in position. I put my hands behind my back, hiding the surprise. Then, as soon as he opens the door, I whip out the shiny, candy-apple-red cylinder, and yell, "Happy birthday!"

A split second later, there's a deafening crack. Confetti shoots into the air and falls all around us, landing in our hair and on our clothes. Jason laughs as he watches the spectacle unfold. Then he pulls me close and kisses my lips as the spring breeze whips up a funnel cloud of tissue paper and glitter. Soon we're surrounded in a beautiful, fluttery mess. It's better than the finale of a Taylor Swift concert.

It's completely magical, and it's completely real.

Acknowledgments

This book would not exist without the keen eye and expert guidance of my brilliant editor, Wendy Loggia. Thank you so much for all your help and support as I worked out the kinks in this story. It has been an honor to work with you.

Jessica Watterson is the best agent an author could ask for: smart, savvy, kind, principled, encouraging, and absolutely badass. Thank you for everything you do to elevate my career. I am so grateful to have you in my corner.

Thank you to the team at Delacorte Press and Underlined for bringing this book to life, and thank you to Sarah Long for the beautiful cover art. Thank you to everyone at Sandra Dijkstra Literary Agency for having my back, with particular thanks to Elise Capron and Andrea Cavallaro.

As I was writing this book, I spent a lot of time thinking about my experiences as a student at Edward R. Murrow High School in Brooklyn, New York. I probably wouldn't have gotten through my senior year without the support of a few amazing teachers. Scott Menscher, John Faciano, and Mollie Spiegel: I'm not sure if you remember me, but your kindness and understanding during the most difficult time of my life had a significant and lasting impact. Thank you for being there for me when I needed it most.

Thanks to everyone who listened to me complain my way through writing this novel: my Slack ladies (Kate, Jordan, Erica, Rosy, Christa, and Lisa), my writer support group (Kathleen, Suzanne, and Chelsea), and my BFFs forever and always, Marci and Jessica.

I listened to *Lover, Red,* and *1989* on repeat for two solid months while I was writing this book, so thanks to Taylor Swift for creating the songs that inspired this story.

Finally, I owe an immense amount of gratitude to my family. Diffy, thanks for keeping me company during all those lonely hours I spend in my office. Andrew, thanks for understanding why I have to spend all those lonely hours in my office when I'd rather be snuggling with you. Emilio, thanks for encouraging me to chase my dreams and for making it possible for me to do so. I love you guys more than anything in this universe.

Don't miss another pitch-perfect
romance from Underlined

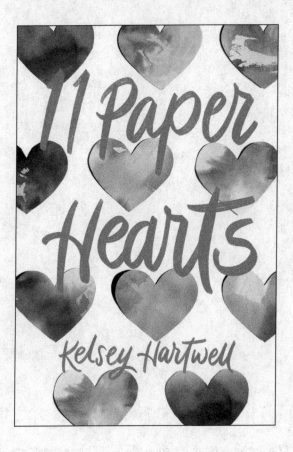

Prologue

I DON'T KEEP MANY SECRETS, BUT THE ONES I DO HAVE ARE hidden underneath a loose floorboard next to my bed.

There are over-the-top diary entries and poems about my deepest crushes—the ones only Carmen knew about. A valentine Adam Gurner gave me in the third grade that I've looked at so many times, I could practically forge his signature. A wrapper from the field trip where Adam offered me a piece of gum. When I got to high school, my secret stash became a little more interesting. There's a birthday card from my first and only boyfriend for my sixteenth birthday signed *Love, Pete.* Every time I look at it, I remember how Carmen squealed because that was the closest thing either of us had heard to *I love you.*

These are just a few of the mementos I keep in my secret

hiding place. No one even knows about the loose floor-board in my room, including my parents, because I hide it under a big fuzzy rug. Whenever I look inside the pocket in my floor, it's a little bit like looking inside my heart. Each item by itself may seem insignificant—but that's the point.

You see, I believe that everyone gets a love story—but you never know when it's going to happen. Like maybe you'll randomly bump into someone at a concert when the band is playing your favorite song. Or maybe you'll lock eyes with some cute stranger across a crowded room. I'm not sure about love at first sight—my mom says true love takes time. But what I do imagine is that you can look back to the moment you met someone you love and think, *yeah, I should've known then.* Because all of your favorite things about them were true then too, staring at you right in the face . . . and you remember how your heart was beating out of your chest. So you decide that it *was* love—the beginning of it—and you just didn't know that yet. Sometimes I think I keep things as simple as a gum wrapper in case these small moments are just the start of something real. Then I can look back and remember everything.

That's what I thought anyways . . . until I had no recollection. There are three things stashed in my hiding place that I don't remember saving:

1. A dried rose
2. A Polaroid of me next to a lamppost, looking
   at the photographer with the biggest smile I've
   ever seen on my face.
3. A bronze key

When I look at these three things, I think maybe I do have more secrets than I thought—even from myself.

Last year I was in an accident coming home from the Valentine's Day Dance at school. It was late at night and snowing the kind of snow that sticks immediately but not bad enough that people say to stay off the streets. I slid off the road on black ice into a tree. But I don't remember this. All I know is what my friends and family have told me and the details that pop up when you google Ella Fitzpatrick.

When I used to search my name to see what college admissions might find, only articles of me volunteering would appear. Now the first thing that comes up in the search engine before I even finish typing is *Ella Fitzpatrick accident.*

I cringe every time.

Because the thing is, when people see the articles, they must see a tragedy. But it wasn't. Not really.

Whenever I feel sorry for myself, I remember I'm lucky for so many reasons. This isn't one of those stories where there was a drunk driver involved or someone with me in the passenger seat died; I'm lucky that Carmen was able to raise money on a GoFundMe account so my family could pay the overwhelming medical bills. Most of all, I'm lucky that my brain bleed stopped when it did.

I even consider myself incredibly lucky for the little things. I'm lucky that I was sixteen and a minor so my picture wasn't plastered on the news. I'm lucky that the accident happened in February, and after my recovery six months later, I was able to make up missed work during summer school so I didn't fall behind. I'm lucky that when I asked to see Pete at the hospital, he came without question even though I had broken up with him three weeks before the accident.

Why couldn't I remember breaking up with him? Well, there were a lot of things I couldn't remember after the accident, like those three items I stored underneath the floorboard.

But I'm also lucky when it comes to my memory loss. Doctors have told me that amnesia is really rare, but when it happens people lose large amounts of time. *Years.* But I only lost a mere two and a half months. Seventy-seven days. Eleven short weeks of my life.

Still, I want to remember. Only whenever I think back to Valentine's Day, my brain feels like it has been bitten into like the end of a lollipop.

But this isn't a tragic story about the eleven weeks I lost.

It's about the eleven paper hearts I discover a year later.

Chapter 1

IT'S THE FIRST FRIDAY OF FEBRUARY AND I KNOW THREE things.

One, Valentine's Day decorations are already up all over school. Red and pink streamers are hung from the ceilings every year to make it feel like love really is in the air. But to me, it screams that love can be torn down at any second.

Two, I miss the days when teachers made everyone from the weird kid that picks his nose in the back of the classroom to your first Top-Secret Crush buy you a valentine. Even though their moms would just buy a pack of generic cards from Target and scribble their names at the bottom, it was something. Now that I don't have a boyfriend, who knows what I'll be getting.

Three, I know my new animosity for Valentine's Day really has nothing to do with these things and everything to do with what happened this time last year.

But I brush that thought aside harder than I brushed the knots out of my hair this morning to make it perfectly straight. Today I'm wearing a printed skirt with a cropped sweater and matching tights. I try to look my best even when I'm not feeling it, which is probably why my friends never know when something is bothering me.

We're huddled together in line for the paper hearts the student government is selling as a fund-raiser for the Valentine's Day Dance. There's a table set up outside the gymnasium, which is the perfect spot because it's where people always hang out before homeroom. A long line has formed from the gym entrance to the boys' locker room around the corner.

There's a part of me that's super proud of the turnout. The paper hearts were my idea in ninth grade when I first joined student government's planning committee. We were trying to think of something original to sell other than carnations to raise money for the Valentine's Day Dance. I thought of love letters immediately. There's something about them that feels so perfectly nostalgic. From there, I thought of selling paper cutouts in the shape of hearts people could write messages on, which would then be passed out around school during the weeks leading up to the dance. You can decorate them and write anything you want to. People mainly send short but sweet ones to their friends. Other times if you're in a relationship you might send a more thoughtful one to show how much you care. What's more romantic than telling someone how you feel?

Ever since freshman year I've gotten a heart from Pete. He isn't the sentimental type, but he always took them seriously. Part of me thinks it's only because it was my idea. But there's another part of me that feels it was genuine—he knew it made me really happy to open one from him.

There's something about receiving love letters that feels way better than some text. I saved all of them in the secret hiding spot next to my bed.

Standing in line, I wonder if any of the paper hearts I get this year will be worth keeping.

"We should get ours for free," Carmen declares as we inch toward the student government table. "Since this was Ella's idea."

Jessica and Katie nod. I glance up at the girl passing out the paper hearts. I forget her name somehow, even though she's the one who always raises her hand in my English class to answer all the questions. I don't really know her personally, but she doesn't exactly scream *rule breaker.*

I shake my head. "Not going to happen. But on the positive side, the money goes toward the dance."

"Oooh. Do you think there's going to be a flower wall for pictures again?" Katie asks.

I blink at the word *again.* I don't remember the flower wall.

Carmen gives Katie a look before answering. "Doubtful. Ella was the only one in student government who actually did anything cool. At least they're doing the paper hearts again instead of passing out dinky carnations. I wouldn't put that past them."

I force a smile like I do a lot lately. I used to *love* being on the planning committee, especially when it came to school dances. One of my favorite things has always been bringing friends together. In middle school, I started organizing big sleepovers complete with games, karaoke sing-offs, and Sephora face masks. They got so popular that my mom had to make me put a cap on who could come. By high school, I graduated to bigger events like school dances as the student body's social chair. But this year I just couldn't bring myself to do it.

"How many hearts do you think I'll get this time?" Jessica asks. "Last year I only got fourteen."

Katie rolls her eyes. "*Only* fourteen? Humble brag a little more, will you."

"Oh, save it," Carmen says. "Besides, paper hearts are about quality over quantity," she says before lightly elbowing me. "Who do you want to get one from?"

I shrug. "I don't even know who I'm sending one to besides you three and Ashley. But she's too cool for school these days. I bet she doesn't even send me one back."

"Forget your sister. What about Pete?" She winks.

I raise my eyebrow. The last person I expect a heart from is my ex-boyfriend, but no matter how many times I insist we're over, she brings him up whenever she can.

"Fine," she says, crossing her arms. "But you better hurry up and think. The line is moving fast."

There's a group of girls in front of us who are chatting excitedly and a boy ahead of them with a super-large backpack. He bounces up and down nervously until the girl from my English class gestures for him to come up to the table and he sprints over. It's endearing and makes me wonder who he's eager to send a note to. Carmen sees too but laughs.

"I have until third period to think about it, remember?" I say, distracting her. "There's a bin outside Principal Wheeler's office for dropping the hearts off."

Carmen's eyes light up. It takes me a second before I realize she's looking over my shoulder. "What about one of them?" she asks, and I turn around to see who she's looking at.

I automatically sigh. Of course it's the boys basketball team—the seniors, anyway, and a couple juniors. Pete's there too.

He always seems to have some sort of radar when I'm nearby, and now is no exception. Pete looks up from a conversation he's having with a guy from the basketball team and spots me across the gymnasium lobby. I might be embarrassed that we made awkward eye contact if it wasn't for the fact that he smiles immediately. I feel my cheeks grow warm, like they did the first time we locked eyes after a game.

After the accident Pete told me he wouldn't get back

together with me since I had broken up with him for a legit reason. Apparently, I had done it because my heart wasn't in it anymore. When Pete told me, he almost started crying like we were breaking up all over again. I realized then how much pain I put him through, even if I couldn't remember it. I vowed to leave him alone after that.

But breakups in high school are strange—you still run into each other and have to wave hello, even though you already said goodbye. When he waves to me now, I smile like I always do as Carmen raises her eyebrow at me.

"You know there *are* other people besides basketball players at the school," I say.

"Like who, *Turtleboy*?" she retorts, looking at the boy who just paid for his paper hearts and is now strapping his big backpack on again. He does kind of look like a turtle. Jessica and Katie laugh as I give an uneasy smile.

"Wait a second," Carmen continues. "Is Sarah Chang *flirting* with Turtleboy?"

I'm not surprised that Carmen's going to continue picking on this poor boy, but I'm surprised that she knows this girl's name. She's not the type to be on Carmen's radar. Maybe she has a class with her? The girl is handing the boy his paper heart and smiling at him—I'd hardly call that flirting. But Jess proudly shows us her phone. She took a photo of the exchange. From the angle, you can barely see the cutout. It looks like they're holding hands.

"Aw, a match made in heaven," Jess says. She even has the perfect rabbit teeth. The tortoise and the hare."

"Oooh. That's a good one." Carmen smiles smugly.

"You guys are terrible," I say, but with not enough force to actually make a difference. I see Jess typing on her phone. Before I can say anything, she looks up and gives a satisfied smile like she does when she posts something.

"So anyway, where are we getting ready for the game tonight?"

My friends start chatting excitedly again, but all I can do is stare at the one heart dangling from the ceiling. It's the same as the others but a little ripped at the bottom. I can't help but feel a little out of place, just like it looks.

Maybe hearts are like paper. Once they are torn, they can never be perfect again.

When I'm up in line, I buy paper hearts for my friends and sister, like I planned, and an extra one for Sarah Chang.